图书在版编目（CIP）数据

孤独是迷人的 /（美）艾米莉·狄金森
（Emily Dickinson）著；苇欢译 . -- 杭州：浙江教育
出版社，2021.12
ISBN 978-7-5722-2578-9

Ⅰ . ①孤… Ⅱ . ①艾… ②苇… Ⅲ . ①诗集—美国—
代 Ⅳ . ① I712.25

中国版本图书馆 CIP 数据核字（2021）第 227609 号

责任编辑　赵露丹　　　美术编辑　韩　波
责任校对　马立改　　　责任印务　时小娟

**孤独是迷人的**
GUDU SHI MIREN DE

［美］艾米莉·狄金森 (Emily Dickinson)　著　　苇　欢　译

出版发行　浙江教育出版社
　　　　　（杭州市天目山路 40 号　电话：0571-85170300-80928）
印　　刷　河北鹏润印刷有限公司
开　　本　787mm×1092mm　1/32
成品尺寸　125mm×185mm
印　　张　13.25
字　　数　131 千字
版　　次　2021 年 12 月第 1 版
印　　次　2021 年 12 月第 1 次印刷
标准书号　ISBN 978-7-5722-2578-9
定　　价　42.00 元

如发现印装质量问题，影响阅读，请与本社市场营销部联系调换。
电话：0571-88909719

磨铁经典第一辑·发光的女性

我要用自己的头脑做武器，
在这艰难的世间开辟出一条路来。

Th
Poem

# "我为美而死"——关于狄金森的诗歌

沈浩波

## 一、她的灵魂是她的侣伴

灵魂选择她自己的侣伴——
然后，关上门——
忠于内心神圣的选择——
不再抛头露面——

不为所动，她看见车辇，停在——
她低矮的门前——
不为所动，即使君王拜倒在
她的石榴裙边——

我了解她，于茫茫人海中——
选择了唯一——
从此心无杂念——
坚如磐石——

这是艾米莉·狄金森写于 1862 年的一首诗，这一年她 32 岁，正处于创作欲望空前旺盛的时期，其写作风格也越来越坚实。狄金森一生存世的作品约 1800 首，写于 1862 年的就多达 366 首。狄金森诗歌的诸多重要元素，如创作风格、美学元素和精神特性，在这一年都已喷薄而出。

这首《灵魂选择她自己的侣伴》(狄金森的原诗并无标题，本文引用的诗歌均为诗人、翻译家苇欢的译本，她以每首诗的第一句作为代标题)就是她的一首典型作品，既体现了狄金森诗歌的精神特性，也展示了其代表性的形式特点和美学风格。

狄金森始终在"向内"写作，在内心世界"发生"诗歌。她的诗歌与 18 世纪和 19 世纪占统治地位的那种表现对外部世界(历史、宗教、人物、爱情、自然)的强烈情感反应的浪漫主义诗歌有本质区别，也与 19 世纪后期法国诗人们通过通感、隐喻和暗示，融合内心世界与外部世界，最终以隐晦神秘的象征方式展现诗人内心隐秘情感的象征主义诗歌大相径庭，当然，与 1920 年以后开始大行其道的现代主义诗歌看起来也不一样(但从更本质的美学特点来说，狄金森提前 60 年进入了现代主义)。狄金森的大部分诗歌，都是直接的、全然的、纯粹的"向内"写作，并不需要过多借助外部世界的象征物。

更为奇特的是，无论是浪漫主义还是象征主义，本质上都是高度抒情化的写作。无论是对外部世界抒情，还是放大和展示内在情感，都是建立在情感、情绪层面上的写作。但狄金森的写作不是，狄金森是在探索、在提问、在试图给出答案、在确认自我。这是一种高度敏感的理性和一种直达本质的感性。

事实上，无论是象征主义的鼻祖波德莱尔[1]，还是与狄金森共同被视为现代主义诗歌先驱的惠特曼[2]，都没有也不可能摆脱浪漫主义风格的烙印。但狄金森很快就摆脱了这种几乎无处不在的影响，并且完全无视了维多利亚时期英语诗歌的所有清规戒律（在这一点上，我甚至相信，她是一个自觉的反叛者）。在 1860 年之后，尤其是进入 1862年之后，她的作品中就已经很少有浪漫主义诗歌的痕迹了。她写出了一种和世界上其他诗歌都不一样的诗歌。这是一个奇迹，在世界诗歌史上绝无仅有。她的很多写法直到 1920 年以后，才被现代主义诗歌的奠基者们，如庞德[3]、W.C. 威廉斯[4] 等人重新发现和倡导。

这种不可思议的独特与狄金森不可思议的生活方式有直接关系。她在 25 岁以后，就过上了闭门不出的幽居生活。在狄金森去世的前五年，她的生命中出现了一个非常重要的女性，名叫梅布尔，是狄金森的哥哥奥斯丁的情人。梅

---

1 夏尔·皮埃尔·波德莱尔（Charles Pierre Baudelaire,1821年—1867年），法国诗人，象征派诗歌之先驱，现代派诗歌之奠基者，散文诗的鼻祖。代表作包括诗集《恶之花》及散文诗集《巴黎的忧郁》。

2 沃尔特·惠特曼（Walt Whitman, 1819年—1892年），美国诗人、散文家、新闻工作者及人文主义者。他身处于超验主义与现实主义间的变革时期，著作兼具两个时期的文风。惠特曼是美国文坛最伟大的诗人之一，有自由诗之父的美誉。他的作品在当时具有争议性，尤其是他的著名诗集《草叶集》。

3 艾兹拉·庞德（Ezra Pound, 1885年—1972年），美国著名诗人、文学家，意象主义诗歌的主要代表人物。

4 威廉·卡洛斯·威廉斯（William Carlos Williams, 1883年—1963年），美国诗人、小说家，庞德的同窗好友。其创作特点是坚持使用口语，简明清晰地描述意象。

布尔仰慕狄金森的才华，经常在狄金森家里为狄金森弹奏钢琴。狄金森静静地坐在二楼的楼梯口倾听，请仆人为梅布尔送一束小花，一笺便条，或者一首抄写的诗。狄金森去世后，梅布尔以狄金森知音好友的身份，费尽心力为狄金森编辑诗集、寻求出版，是狄金森诗歌得以传播的第一功臣。但她始终觉得尴尬的是，她们相处了五年，一直在灵魂层面沟通，甚至同处一屋，却从来没有见过面。幽居得如此彻底，若无非凡之灵魂怎么可能？

狄金森在她二楼的房间写诗，写字的桌子就摆在窗前。桌子很小，只够放一张信纸。透过窗子，能看到家里的花园。花园里，有她侄子和侄女小时候奔跑的情景。据她的表妹路易莎·诺克斯回忆，很多时候，狄金森喜欢在厨房的储藏室里写诗。这就是狄金森 25 岁之后生活和思考的世界。很幽闭吗？往外部世界看，的确如此。但是狄金森却把目光更专注地朝向了"内部"，朝向了"灵魂"，这灵魂的内部因此便扩展成了一个世界，一个生动的、雀跃的世界。

狄金森好奇地探究着这个世界的一切真相。她有无数的疑问，并尝试对这些疑问做出回答。她是这个世界唯一的居民，是唯一的提问者，也是唯一的回答者。不是所有问题都有答案，但无论她是否犹疑不决、苦恼困惑，无论是肯定的答案还是否定的答案，都直接构成了诗。没有比这样的诗歌更坚决的诗歌，她不是写给任何其他人看的，丝毫不需要矫饰和表演。这是最诚实的诗歌，抵达生命之真实。

《灵魂选择她自己的侣伴》正是这样的诗。狄金森并不孤独，她拥有自己的灵魂——这忠贞的、坚如磐石的侣伴。狄金森在"向内"的凝视中，看到了自己的灵魂，看到了灵魂和自己的关系。

狄金森这种"向内"的写作，必然使得她的写作主题高度形而上，高度抽象。但她在处理这些形而上的、抽象的概念和主题时，体现了高度创造性的写作智慧——她用非常先进的写作技术解决了形而上写作容易流于空泛和虚浮的难题。《灵魂选择她自己的侣伴》，就展现了其高超技艺中的一种——将抽象具体化，赋予形而上以形而下的身体。

"灵魂"，本是一个形而上的抽象概念，在诗中却成了一个独立的人格体。她把灵魂直接当成了一个活生生的人。当灵魂成为一个鲜活的"人"，就拥有了情感、动作、情境、场景，抽象瞬间变得具体。这使得狄金森的形而上主题没有陷入高蹈和漂浮，而是变得清晰、可把握。如此高超而现代的诗歌技法，出现在 1862 年，一个当时无人知晓的女诗人的某张便笺上。洞悉诗歌写作秘密的人，会知道这是多么神奇的创造。

在 1861 年，狄金森即写过一首以"希望"这一抽象名词为主题的诗，采用的是同样的技法：

"希望"长着翅膀——

栖落在灵魂深处——

唱一曲无言的歌——

永不停歇，永不——

狂风中听见，悠扬的乐曲——
咆哮的风暴——
让这只小鸟进退两难
它温暖过许多人——

我曾听见它的歌，在最寒冷的地方——
在最偏僻的海上——
然而，身逢绝境，
它也不曾，向我索要一颗米粮。


正因为狄金森有"灵魂"这一坚定的侣伴，所以她永远能听到"希望"的鸟儿在心中歌唱。这使得她虽然幽居在家，足不出户，却并没有将自己的写作变得幽闭和枯索。恰恰相反，她的写作总体上倾向于开阔和明亮，饱含着对人世的情感和对生活的热爱。而在这首《"希望"长着翅膀》中，"希望"鲜活得如此具体，因为狄金森真的听到和看到了它。

狄金森是现代主义诗歌的先驱，当我惊艳于她如此天然而高超地在诗歌中表现抽象与具体时，不由想起了现代主义绘画的先驱塞尚。他也是一位孤僻的怪人，在其后半生的创作中，同样以惊人的方式处理了抽象与具体的关系。

## 二、她的内在是一座剧场

我看不见路，天堂被缝起——
我感到门柱在闭合——
地球颠倒了两极——
我触摸宇宙——

它接着向后滑，我独自一人——
如球体上的斑点——
在圆周上行走——
听不到半点钟声——

这首诗的核心要素是什么？是意象和事件。它像不像一出现代派的戏剧？由短短八行构建的戏剧，一幕完全的"内心戏"。在狄金森此刻的内心里，有天堂——具体的天堂，有具体的形状，被缝起的天堂，门柱在闭合；有地球，颠倒了两极的地球；更有宇宙，具体的宇宙，宇宙在向后滑。狄金森将她的恐惧感真实地写成了具体的内心事件。这种将内在的情感意象化、形象化、场景化、事件化甚至戏剧化的表达方式，在狄金森的诗歌里比比皆是。通过意象和事件来呈现诗意，对狄金森来说，已经是写作的常识——而世界诗歌对此的认知，还要到下一个世纪才出现。

狄金森运用的这种写作方式，已经不仅仅是处理抽象与具象的关系了，不仅仅是给情感赋形了，而是它还使情感成为事件，成为戏剧。这种美学，直到 21 世纪的今天，依然显得先进。

1862 年，狄金森曾经做过唯一的一次尝试，试图与外部的诗歌世界"发生关系"。她将几首诗歌寄给当时的一位文学专家——希金森。后世研究者普遍认为，这是狄金森对于自己的创作初具自信后，希望发表自己诗歌的一次努力。但这遭到了希金森严苛的批评，希金森认为她的诗歌缺乏控制，并建议她不要急着发表。好一个缺乏控制，狄金森当然不会允许其作品像彼时在美国占绝对主流地位的那些平庸诗歌一样受制于种种清规戒律，她生来就是陈腐美学的反抗者；好一个不要急着发表，从此狄金森就再也没有寻求过发表，直到去世。

这是一次典型的明珠暗投，是平庸者对天才的无法理解。最初读到这个典故时，我也曾在心里怒骂希金森之蒙昧昏庸，让狄金森未能更早地为世人所知，未能更早地对世界诗歌产生影响。但我当然也明白，一个诗人过于领先于时代，无论如何她都将注定孤独。就算希金森真将她的诗推荐或发表于杂志，又能怎样？被讥讽和嘲弄恐怕才是常态。尝试失败后的狄金森从此更坚定地摈弃了她的时代，决绝而纯粹地沉浸于自己的内心，遵循自身创造的美学，这才缔造了世界诗歌史上惊人的奇迹。

狄金森终其一生，未与外部的诗歌世界发生碰撞。她所创造的诗歌美学，要等去世后很多年，才会令世人惊叹。直到 20 世纪初，现代派诗歌的肇始流派意象派才令此后的美国诗歌始终围绕"意象"展开，其核心诗人庞德则在意象派的宣言文章《几条戒律》的第一条就提出"直接描写客观事物"，这才令诗歌真正进入到突出具体性的时代，避免了诗歌语言的一味抽象空洞、漂浮、缺乏承载和质感。到了1946年，现代派诗歌的另一位重要奠基者W.C.威廉斯，在对诗歌的思考完全成熟以后，才提出了他最重要的主张"不表现观念，只描写事物"，意思是诗人不要对其所想表达的情感、思想、理念进行言说，强加给读者。观念本身不是诗，言说也不是诗。通过对具体事物的描写呈现出诗意，才是诗。诗在具体的事物中。这虽然是对意象派诗歌和庞德早期诗歌主张的再次确认和发展，却依然成为对20世纪下半叶的现代主义诗歌来说最具纲领意义的诗学观念。庞德和W.C.威廉斯所强调的"事物"是指外部世界的事物，而狄金森将其心灵内部的抽象世界完全转化为可见、可触的意象和事件，我以为后者更具天才的创造性。

我当然知道不应该跨越时代和历史情境去比较狄金森的写作和庞德、W.C.威廉斯等人的主张之间的高下。事实上，W.C.威廉斯身上有更尖锐和广阔的先锋性。但我还是特别想指出一点，在庞德和威廉斯所提及的"事物"这一概念中，他们往往更侧重于作为意象之"物"，相比之下，狄金森写作中所呈现出的那种明显的"事件化"，我以为尤其显得超前。

狄金森诗歌里的这种事件化，不同于西方诗歌中一直都有的那种冗长拖沓的"叙事诗"传统。"叙事诗"传统源自史诗，更强调的是"叙事"这一功能，并非基于纯粹的"诗"的意义。狄金森诗歌中的这种事件性、戏剧性，乃是通过具象方式呈现抽象之"诗"的美学手段，是纯诗范畴内的美学，而不是功能。

狄金森往往能在非常简洁的诗歌空间里，呈现内心世界里的事件风暴和戏剧场景。《我看不见路，天堂被缝起》只有八行，却拥有巨大的戏剧空间和诗性空间。她的另一首名作《我为美而死》也有同样的效果：

我为美而死，却还不能
适应坟墓
一个为真理而死的人
正躺在我的隔壁——

他轻声地问，"你为何而死？"
"为了美。"我回答——
"我，为真理，它们本是一体——
我们，是同胞。"他说——

就这样，像亲人，重逢在夜里——
我们隔墙而谈——
直到青苔爬上我们的嘴唇——
覆盖我们的姓名——

在这首诗中，狄金森精心设计了一幕场景，在十二行的空间里，构建了丰富、复杂、微妙的转折和变化。她在心灵深处搭建了舞台，布置了场景，形成了事件，托举起诗意。死亡之幻灭，美和真理之甘甜，这中间的张力，构成了诗歌。"我为美而死"是一句"诗言志"，"言志"不是诗，如同格言、警句、表决心都不是诗一样。但紧接着"却还不能适应坟墓"，立刻就开始转向场景，帷幕拉开，诗就开始了。

为美而死的"我"，和为真理而死的"他"，在死亡的黑暗中相遇，彼此验证着美和真理的甘甜，互相给予对方面对死亡之幻灭的勇气。这幕戏剧里有美好、有犹疑、有孤独、有坚定、有幻灭、有温暖。这些复杂、深刻、丰富而又微妙的感觉，如何言说？无法言说。而诗正是不可言说的，将不可言说的东西呈现出来才是诗，这呈现的过程才是诗。

长期幽居、孤身一人、专注于内在的狄金森有着极其丰富而纤微的内心，有着时时刻刻的内心起伏。每一次起伏，都是一场内心的戏剧，狄金森既是演出者，又是观赏者。正如她自己在诗中写道：

演出永无穷尽
在人们心中——
这唯一有史记载的剧场
主人无法关闭——

而她又有那么天才的、凝练而简洁的写作能力，将这些或轻微或澎湃的起伏，或复杂或神秘的戏剧，展现在一首首短诗里。与她相比，后世现代主义的那些不写出一首长诗，好像就无法展示其深邃复杂，无法在诗坛获得影响力的诗人——对，我说的就是艾略特、庞德、W.C.威廉斯等人，显得多么世故、功利而浅薄。

生命、死亡、宗教、永恒、不朽、灵魂、希望、恐慌、焦虑……还有爱情，狄金森将这一切形而上的抽象思考，全都具象为诗，具象为心灵的事件、内在的戏剧。尤其是爱情。狄金森的爱情经历虽然已经被后世的研究者从极少的证据中反复考证，仍然难以确切，但又何必考证得那么确切呢？她为我们留下了那么多爱情之诗！在狄金森所有内心的戏剧风暴中，最令我读得惊心动魄的，正是一首爱情诗，这首诗甚至有很强的身体感：

> 他摸索你的灵魂
>
> 像乐师抚摸琴键
>
> 然后奏响完整的乐章——
>
> 他逐渐让你惊叹——
>
> 为你脆弱的天性做好防备
>
> 迎接超凡的一击
>
> 以音槌轻轻击打——
>
> 由远及近，徐徐而来
>
> 等你的呼吸得到平复——
>
> 头脑慢慢冷静——
>
> 再向你施以威严的霹雳——
>
> 把你裸露的灵魂剥去外皮——

当风的巨手摇撼森林——
宇宙寂然无声——


## 三、她的生命是一滴琼浆

有些人守安息日去教堂——
而我，在家里守——
用一只长刺歌雀唱诗——
果园，就是穹顶——


有些人守安息日身穿白袍——
而我只佩戴翅膀——
没有教堂的，鸣钟，
我们的小司事——歌唱。


上帝传道，他是知名的牧师——
这训诫从来不长久，
我最终，没有去天堂——
我一直在，行路。


放在 19 世纪的美国新英格兰地区，这几乎是一首无所
畏惧的离经叛道之诗。她心中另有教堂，她自己就是天使，
上帝的训诫对她无效，宗教所描绘的天堂不是她的理想之
所，她选择行走在人间的路上。"我一直在，行路"，她更
忠实于生命的过程。

狄金森所居住的阿姆斯特小镇，恪守着严苛保守的清教徒传统。而且其时美国正在经历一场亢奋激进的宗教复兴运动，人们被号召在各种公开场合下宣称自己的信仰与得救。狄金森的整个家族都素以虔诚著称，举家积极参与这场运动。狄金森就读的霍利约克女子学院，几乎是一座按照宗教律条运行的学校。即使在这样的环境下，狄金森也没有选择皈依正教。在学校，她被视为"不可救药"的学生；在家里，她是唯一的非基督教徒。如此巨大的压力，少女时代的狄金森到底是如何承受的？她该有着多么强大的绝不屈从的心性？

这种天生的怀疑主义是她成为一个诗人的最坚实的心灵基础，并由此生长出狄金森始终恪守真实、探寻真理的倾向，一生不懈地对生命、死亡、不朽、永恒进行追问。她因此有着全然独立的灵魂和叛逆不屈的文学个性。所以这样一个人，一旦成为诗人，怎么可能会被那个时代浮夸腐朽又充满清规戒律的主流诗歌所束缚呢？她必将创造出只属于自己的诗歌，必将成为19世纪最伟大的创造者。

一方面，狄金森怀疑被人们所传播的天堂是否存在，质疑和挑战上帝的权威；另一方面，无处不在的宗教环境和从小熟读的《圣经》，又让她一生都在思考《圣经》所提出的各种形而上的终极命题。她不屈从于上帝，但又对上帝充满好奇，她以一颗自由无羁的天真之心去接近那个名为上帝的存在。某些时候，她在讥诮：

我当然祈祷过——

可上帝在乎吗?

在他眼中这不过是

空中的鸟,跺了跺脚——

大喊着"给我"——

生存的理由——

……


有时候,她又开起了轻盈的玩笑,仿佛上帝是她的一个朋友:


篱笆那边——

种着草莓——

篱笆那边——

我能翻过去,一试便知——

草莓多可口!


可是弄脏了围裙——

上帝一定会将我责怪!

哦,亲爱的,我猜,假如他是个孩子——

他也会翻过去,如果他可以!


还有这一首:


上帝真是一个好嫉妒的神——

他无法忍受

我们将他晾在一边

彼此间却玩得不亦乐乎。


狄金森与上帝之间，几乎是平等的，这令她的心灵自由而活泼。在她的眼中，上帝有各种各样的形态，这些诗幽默而生动。是的，在很多时候，狄金森都是一个幽默的诗人，甚至是一个爱在诗中开点儿玩笑的诗人。太现代了，是不是？她哪里像是19世纪的诗人？别以为她是一个板着面孔的老处女，不，她非常鲜活，有着超越世纪的那种鲜活，指向永恒。

在狄金森的所有诗中，死亡、宗教和爱情是她着力最多的三大主题。而死亡主题从某种程度来说，其实也是对宗教主题的延展。但不同的是，狄金森在处理那些更直接的宗教主题时，心态非常放松，写得自由活泼，花样百出，有否定、有质疑、有讥诮、有玩笑。而一旦进入死亡主题，或者有关死亡的宗教主题，我们往往就能体会到狄金森内心最严峻的时刻。我从来没有见过像狄金森这样醉心于想象死亡、思考死亡的诗人，从年轻到迟暮，她一直在书写死亡。

年轻时她更多的是在想象死亡，无论如何想象，死亡总是那么令人恐惧和惊慌，意味着黑暗和虚无。但是狄金森绝不甘心陷入虚无和黑暗，她必须找到另外的答案。但这太难了，如同她在《因为我无法驻足等候死神》一诗的结尾所发出的惊呼。她终于意识到，死亡比生命更指向永恒。死亡如此永恒，而生命如同露珠，如何自处？又如同她在《我见过一只垂死的眼睛》里所揭示的，"曾经看见是一种恩赐"，但死亡终于让死者紧紧阖上眼睛，他被剥夺了这恩赐。生命是一种恩赐，而死亡又将这恩赐剥夺。但狄金森仍然不肯放弃对死亡的思考，随着她越来越确认死亡的属性，她的诗歌甚至变得紧张而凶猛，带着愤怒的决绝：

那时，垂死之人，

清楚自己要去何处——

他们来到上帝的右手边——

那只手已被截断

上帝也不知所终——


放弃信仰

让行动变得渺小——

一点磷火照耀

胜过一片漆黑——


　　这首诗大约写于 1882 年，那年她 52 岁，离去世还有四年。她已经更加笃定地得到了关于死亡的答案。没有救赎、没有拯救、没有复活，上帝的右手已被截断，上帝不在了。上帝的右手边在基督教中被视为最荣耀之地，复活升天的耶稣就坐在上帝的右边，因此虔诚的基督徒们相信他们死后，将作为得救者，与耶稣一起坐在上帝的右手边，并得以复活。

这首诗的第一段写得凌厉凶悍，直接宣布，上帝的右手已被截断。这身体性极强的语言，显露出了某种决绝。她终于彻底解决了她和上帝的关系，也因此解决了她和死亡的关系。在死亡的阴影已经开始笼罩她的生命时，狄金森已心如磐石，知道自己无论如何也不可能因为对死亡的恐惧而臣服。这一段诗歌是狄金森所有死亡主题诗歌中最璀璨的华章，她通过对死亡的确认，获得了个人生命意志的最大舒张。

这首诗的第二段有些令人费解。"放弃信仰／让行动（或者说是行为）变得渺小——"也有译者没有采用"渺小"这一译法，而是采用"卑微"一词。"行动变得卑微"，对后两句就有了很强的否定性。而"渺小"则显得中性了很多。"一点磷火照耀／胜过一片漆黑"到底是指什么？我更愿意信任此处我所引用的诗人、翻译家苇欢的翻译理解——放弃了信仰，也即放弃了宗教对于生命和死亡的宏大叙事，放弃了崇高的天国叙事，回到人的渺小。而人死后，哪怕永不得救，哪怕灵魂消逝分散，肉身变成一点磷火，也能照耀永恒的黑暗。有译者将磷火理解成人们失去信仰后追逐各种歪门邪道的"鬼火"，与"卑微"的行为相对应。看似也说得通，但我觉得这恐怕是对狄金森的过度解读。狄金森的诗歌其实非常直接，她不怎么在语言上玩儿虚的。她就是主动放弃了信仰，回到了人的肉身，接受了生命的衰亡。但哪怕只剩"一点磷火"，也是生命曾经存在的证据，这磷火在黑暗中闪耀，带着生命存在过的骄傲。

如果说这"一点磷火"，是以一种决绝的姿态，从死亡的方向反证生命的意义。那么，在她的另一首有可能写于1862年的诗——《我啜饮过生活的甘醇》中，"一滴琼浆"的意象正好可以用来作为对照：

我啜饮过生活的甘醇——
并告诉你我的代价——
不多不少，用尽一生——
这是市价，他们说。

他们精微地测量过我——
锱铢较量，分毫不差，
再赐予我我生命之分量——
一滴天堂的琼浆！

研究狄金森诗歌的权威学者、《艾米莉·狄金森诗全集》的编辑托马斯·约翰逊猜测这首诗可能写于1862年，但他也不是很拿得准。从这首诗里对"天堂"的某种还算认可的态度来看，好像确实是她更年轻时的作品；但从这首诗里那种过尽千帆的人生感来讲，又有点像其晚年的作品。在我看来，这里的"天堂"其实带有某种讥诮的讽刺感，所以我更倾向于这是狄金森较晚时期的诗歌。

这首诗体现了狄金森高度的生命理性与智性，同时又展现了其浓郁的生命感性。她理智而冷酷地揭示了人获得美好生命的代价，上帝锱铢必较地为每个人确认好了价格，这价格就是人的一生。作为交易物，上帝会用死亡将其收割走。生命是一滴琼浆，但这天堂恩赐的琼浆却是用人生最终会被交付给死亡为代价的。如果仅仅看到这一层，那么这是一首冷酷而讥诮的诗。但狄金森的高妙之处在于，这首诗如同一场永无止境的正反循环，或者说，如同拥有正反两面的镜子，它的另一面则是，即便我们最终将交付出整个人生，即使付出这样的代价，但毕竟，我们也啜饮过生活的甘醇。死亡是生命的代价，但生命是一滴琼浆。

"一点磷火"——生命之于死亡；"一滴琼浆"——也是生命之于死亡。在狄金森对死亡的反复书写中，她其实更确证了生命的意义。她的叛逆、独立、自由、反抗，都构成了生命的甘醇，确证了生命的价值，进而展示了生而为人的意义。

狄金森临死前，曾坚定地要求她的妹妹将她所写的一切字纸全部烧掉。但她的妹妹没有遵从她的旨意，在烧毁了她的大部分信件后，留下了她所有的诗歌。于是，这个一直在想象、思考和面对死亡的女诗人，最终以另一种方式获得了永生。

狄金森入殓时，她的挚友和知音——她的嫂子苏姗，为她缝制了一件白色法兰绒袍子，在她的颈边摆放杓兰和紫罗兰；她的妹妹拉维妮娅将两枝紫色的天芥菜花放在姐姐手里；特地前来参加葬礼的，她长期通信的笔友希金森在日记里写道：她好像神奇地回到了青春时代，回到了她的三十岁，没有白发也没有皱纹，显得美丽而安宁；一位出现在葬礼上的小女孩，长大后回忆说：葬礼那天，空气中飘荡着苹果花的味道，狄金森躺在小巧的棺木里……

一切都很美好，她的生命是一滴琼浆。

## 四、她的诗歌是一场革命

制造一片草原，需要一株三叶草和一只蜜蜂，

一株三叶草，一只蜜蜂，

还有白日梦。

白日梦就够了，

假如连蜜蜂也没有。

这是一首美丽而精致的小诗。是一首没有任何抒情语言，没有任何抽象语言，没有任何形容词，没有任何修辞，没有任何说教，没有讲任何道理的诗。即使放到今天，它也足以构成一种诗学层面上的高级感。这首诗到底写于哪一年已不可考，但不管写于何时，在19世纪中后期的美国，乃至整个英语诗歌界，出现这样的诗歌都显得过于超前。就好像在一群穿着紧得勒死人的束腰和曳地长裙的中世纪贵妇中间，突然冒出了一个从20世纪的海滨沙滩上穿越过来的女郎，健康的肌肤上，滚落的水珠闪闪发光。

五行，四个意象，两次转折，一个神来之笔，构成了一首精妙的意象纯诗。它几乎符合20世纪初意象派诗人们所提出的各种美学原则。使用日常的语言，明晰而具体，直接用意象构成诗歌，没有任何抽象空洞的语言或议论，

诗意高度浓缩而简洁，形式自由。难怪20世纪的美国诗人路易斯·昂特米尔[1]读完狄金森后惊呼："在意象派成为口号的50多年前，狄金森在没有任何声张的情况下，实现了意象写作……各种预示着现代性的表现手法，在狄金森的诗歌中，像证据一样随处可见。"

狄金森于1862年左右创作的另一首诗，就已将意象主义的手段运用得炉火纯青，正如昂特迈耶所说，诗中到处闪烁着现代主义诗歌精神的光芒：

一只鸟，飞落在小路上——
并不知道我在一旁——
看它将一只虫子啄成两半
再生吞下肚，

接着，它在近旁的草叶上
啜饮一滴露水——
又轻跃到墙边
给一只甲虫让路——

它飞快地转转眼珠
茫然环顾四周——
像两颗惊恐的珠子，我这样想——

---

1  路易斯·昂特米尔（Louis Untermeyer，1885年—1977年），美国诗人、文选学家、评论家和编辑。

它晃着丝绒般的小脑袋

仿佛身处危险，小心翼翼，
我丢给它一块面包屑
它便舒展羽毛
拍拍翅膀飞回了家——

比船桨拨开海水更温柔，
银色的海面没有波澜——
比正午飞离沙洲的蝴蝶更轻盈
不溅起一朵浪花。

　　一只鸟，把一只虫子啄成两半，再生吞下肚——这是诗，生命的生动即是诗；它啜饮一滴露水，给一只甲虫让路——这是诗，生命微妙的行为即是诗；它舒展羽毛飞走，像船桨拨开海水，不溅起空气的浪花——这是诗，狄金森用语言呈现出生命之美。起源于意象派，经过庞德和W.C. 威廉斯的反复树立，从而成为20世纪统治现代主义诗歌的核心观点：事物本身就是诗。在狄金森的这首诗中，早就暗自散发着新的美学原则的光芒。这种意象主义的典范作品，狄金森写过不少，但她并未，也不可能在这个方向过多发展。因为作为一名幽居者，她并没有机会与这个世界上更多的事物相遇。真正属于她的诗歌，依然是内在的、形而上层面的灵魂追问。
　　她只是早已洞悉事物本身自有诗性，早就创造出通过意象呈现诗意的技术——这同时也构成了她形而上写作的巨大原创性，她观察和写作内在的心灵世界如同观察和写作事物本身，她能将主观客观化，能将抽象形象化。在19世纪，她创造出了一种全新的诗歌之美。不是与她同时代的法国象征主义诗人们所推崇的"唯美"——那种夸张矫饰的神秘颓废，仿佛高烧患者和肺炎患者脸上病态的鲜红，而是一种真实、健康、朴素、明晰、生动的生命之美。

发轫于1908年左右，在1914年到1917年达到顶峰的意象派诗歌，最早就是由七八位充满革新精神的英美年轻诗人发起创作的。庞德是其中的核心人物，日后大名鼎鼎的美国女诗人希尔达·杜利特尔[1]和英国诗人、小说家D.H.劳伦斯都在其中。意象派诗歌运动作为现代主义诗歌运动的第一声炮响，包含着明确的抗争和反对。他们的每一条主张，都在反对在当时占统治地位的英美旧诗歌的美学，同时力求建立起崭新的美学。他们反对那种夸张矫饰的抒情、无病呻吟的自我哀怜、假大空的议论和说教、清教徒式森严的格律规范……现代主义者们对旧的美学系统进行的是一场决裂式的革命，比法国的象征主义诗人们要坚决得多。

而狄金森则在约50年前，一个人静悄悄地走上了这条反对和决裂之路。这是诗歌史上最温和的一场革命。它所吹起的风暴甚至没有离开过狄金森窗前那张小小的书桌，她的"敌人"们对此一无所知。后世的诗人和研究者，却

---

1  希尔达·杜利特尔（Hilda Doolittle或H.D.，1886年—1961年），美国诗人、小说家，以20世纪初期与意象派诗人埃兹拉·庞德、理查德·奥尔丁顿等人的交往而知名。希尔达后来的诗作吸收了意象派的美学，但更具有女性主义的特色。

纷纷从狄金森留下的诗歌中，震惊于她在这场战斗中所取得的胜利。哈罗德·布罗姆甚至说："除莎士比亚之外，狄金森所表现出的认知的原创性超过了但丁以来的所有西方诗人……这是400年来西方诗人中绝无仅有的。"

狄金森何以创造出这样的诗歌之美？何以具备如此强大的美学原创性？我以为这来自其始终求真和始终追求灵魂自由的天性。

正如她在《我为美而死》一诗中所揭示的。"为美而死"和"为真理而死"，诗中的"Truth"一词，既可以翻译成"真理"，也可以翻译成"真"。在汉语里，"真理"和"真"有着不同的指向。"我为美而死"，"我为真而死"，这两者更能构成一种本质的呼应。因为"真"，所以"美"。狄金森也确实是一个始终求真的诗人，她的所有诗歌都指向诚实，指向真实。她既有怀疑主义者的求真的天性，又深知真实本身的力量。"为美而死""为真而死""它们本是一体"，道尽了真与美的关系，真即是美，美即是真。

她是求真者，也是追求灵魂自由者。而她确实也是自由的。幽居的生活看似牢牢束缚住了她的身体，但没有任何东西可以阻挡和绑架她的灵魂。名利的诱惑、世俗的偏见、信仰的控制、文化的秩序、文学的权力……所有这些都与她无关。1862年之后，她就再也没有渴望过发表，没有渴望过被现世认可；临死之前，她让妹妹烧掉所有她写下的东西。她甚至不打算追求身后之名。她获得了最大的心灵自由。

而对于真实和自由的追求，不正是所有文学革命和艺术革命最本质的动力吗？不正是现代主义诗歌所追求的美学理想吗？因此狄金森的写作，乃是一颗真实的灵魂、一具鲜活的生命全然按照自己心意的绽放。她创造了新的美学，写出了一个完整的生命。

"我为美而死"——正是如此。

2021.7.18

（说明：本文引用的诗歌都引自诗人、翻译家苇欢的译本。没有她所翻译的这些诗歌，我根本就没有办法真正接近狄金森。苇欢的翻译既明晰，又富有诗性，是国内不可多得的狄金森译本。）

# 希望长着翅膀

# 这是我写给世界的信

# 我曾啜饮生活的甘醇

希望长着翅膀

## 0004

## 在这神奇的海上

在这神奇的海上——
默默航行
呵！舵手，呵！
你可知道岸的方向
哪里没有嘶吼的碎浪——
风暴在何处停歇？

宁静的西方
落下，片片风帆——
船已抛锚停泊——
我要将你引向那里——
登上，呵！
不朽的彼岸！

0004

## On this wondrous sea

On this wondrous sea—
Sailing silently,
Ho! Pilot, ho!
Knowest thou the shore
Where no breakers roar—
Where the storm is o'er?

In the peaceful West
Many the sails at rest—
The anchors fast—
Thither I pilot thee—
Land Ho! Eternity!
Ashore at last!

## 有一个词

有一个词
词里藏剑
能刺穿手持武器之人——
它抛出锋利的音节
又再度沉默——
被拯救的人会说出
它在哪里倒下
在爱国日,
某个佩戴肩章的弟兄
停止了呼吸。

无论悄无声息的太阳在何处奔跑——
无论白日在何处漫步——
它在发动无声的进攻——
它获得胜利!
看啊, 这最敏锐的神枪手!
最精准的一射!
时间最崇高的目标
是被"遗忘"的灵魂!

## There is a word

There is a word
Which bears a sword
Can pierce an armed man—
It hurls its barbed syllables
And is mute again—
But where it fell
The saved will tell
On patriotic day,
Some epauletted Brother
Gave his breath away.

Wherever runs the breathless sun—
Wherever roams the day—
There is its noiseless onset—
There is its victory!
Behold the keenest marksman!
The most accomplished shot!
Time's sublimest target
Is a soul "forgot!"

## 晨光比从前更温柔

晨光比从前更温柔——
褐色的毛栗快要成熟——
浆果的脸蛋更加丰润——
玫瑰在室外盛开。

枫树抖动明艳的纱巾——
田野披上红袍——
我生怕自己显得过时
只好别上一枚饰针。

**0012**

## The morns are meeker than they were

The morns are meeker than they were—
The nuts are getting brown—
The berry's cheek is plumper—
The Rose is out of town.

The Maple wears a gayer scarf—
The field a scarlet gown—
Lest I should be old fashioned
I'll put a trinket on.

## 一片花萼，一枚花瓣，一根刺

一个寻常夏日的清晨——
一片花萼，一枚花瓣，一根刺
一瓶露水，两只蜜蜂——
一阵清风，鸟在林间雀跃——
而我，一朵玫瑰！

0019

## A sepal, petal, and a thorn

A sepal, petal, and a thorn
Upon a common summer's morn—
A flask of Dew—A Bee or two—
A Breeze—a caper in the trees—
And I'm a Rose!

## 我们输了，因为我们赢了

我们输了，因为我们赢了——
赌徒们，铭记于心
并再一次掷出骰子！

0021

## We lose—because we win

We lose—because we win—
Gamblers—recollecting which
Toss their dice again!

## 假如记忆就是遗忘

假如记忆就是遗忘，
我便再也想不起
假如遗忘就是记忆，
我几乎就要忘却。
假如思念就是快乐，
哀痛就是喜悦，
手指多么欢快
今朝将此采撷！

0033

## If recollecting were forgetting

If recollecting were forgetting,
Then I remember not
And if forgetting, recollecting,
How near I had forgot.
And if to miss, were merry,
And to mourn, were gay,
How very blithe the fingers
That gathered this, Today!

## 没有人知道这朵小玫瑰

没有人知道这朵小玫瑰——
若不是我将它从道旁摘下
捧起它献给你
它或许是一位朝圣者
只有蜜蜂会思念它——
只有蝴蝶,
长途奔忙——
只为在它的胸脯上停歇——
只有鸟儿感到疑惑——
只有微风不住叹息——
啊,像你这样的,小玫瑰
多么轻易就凋谢!

## Nobody knows this little Rose

Nobody knows this little Rose—
It might a pilgrim be
Did I not take it from the ways
And lift it up to thee
Only a Bee will miss it—
Only a Butterfly,
Hastening from far journey—
On its breast to lie—
Only a Bird will wonder—
Only a Breeze will sigh—
Ah Little Rose—how easy
For such as thee to die!

## 那样惨痛的损失我已经历两次

那样惨痛的损失我已经历两次。
如今都已入土。
我曾两次形同乞丐
站在上帝门前!

天使,曾两次下凡
赔偿我的损失——
窃贼! 银行家,父亲!
我又一次穷困不堪!

0049

# I never lost as much but twice

I never lost as much but twice,
And that was in the sod.
Twice have I stood a beggar
Before the door of God!

Angels—twice descending
Reimbursed my store—
Burglar! Banker—Father!
I am poor once more!

## 假如我死去

假如我死去，
你仍活着——
时间流逝——
清晨会散发光芒——
正午的阳光炽烈燃烧——
一如往常——
假如鸟儿仍早起筑巢
蜜蜂来去奔忙——
一个人也可以选择
长眠地下！
多么美好，当我们伴着雏菊躺下
市场依旧坚挺——
商业与贸易，从容进展——
充满朝气——
这一切让离别变得宁静
灵魂充满安详——
瞧，那位先生正欢快地
做着生意！

## If I should die

If I should die,
And you should live—
And time should gurgle on—
And morn should beam—
And noon should burn—
As it has usual done—
If Birds should build as early
And Bees as bustling go—
One might depart at option
From enterprise below!
'Tis sweet to know that stocks will stand
When we with Daisies lie—
That Commerce will continue—
And Trades as briskly fly—
It makes the parting tranquil
And keeps the soul serene—
That gentlemen so sprightly
Conduct the pleasing scene!

## 从未成功过的人们

从未成功过的人们
才会认为成功最甜美。
甘露的滋味
需要最迫切的渴求方能体会。

今日的胜利之师
没有人能高扬凯旗
清晰地阐释
胜利

奄奄一息的，战败者——
即将失去听觉的耳朵
听见远方激昂的凯歌
悲痛而嘹亮！

0067

**Success is counted sweetest**

Success is counted sweetest
By those who ne'er succeed.
To comprehend a nectar
Requires sorest need.

Not one of all the purple Host
Who took the Flag today
Can tell the definition
So clear of Victory

As he defeated—dying—
On whose forbidden ear
The distant strains of triumph
Burst agonized and clear!

## 去天堂吧！

去天堂吧！

不知何时——

别问我怎样祈祷！

我的确过于惊讶

反倒不知如何回答！

去天堂吧！

这听起来多么渺茫！

但我们一定能到达

像夜晚归家的牧群

回到牧羊人的怀抱！


或许你也在路上！

谁知道呢？

假如你先抵达

帮我留一寸地方就好

紧靠着我失去的那两个人——

最小的"长袍"就合我身

再戴一小顶"花冠"——

因为你知道回家时

我们不必介意自己的着装——

我高兴我不相信天堂
它会让我停止呼吸——
我还想再看一看
如此奇妙的大地!
我高兴他们对此深信不疑
在那个盛大的秋日午后
我将他们埋葬
此后再也找寻不到。

## Going to Heaven!

Going to Heaven!
I don't know when—
Pray do not ask me how!
Indeed I'm too astonished
To think of answering you!
Going to Heaven!
How dim it sounds!
And yet it will be done
As sure as flocks go home at night
Unto the Shepherd's arm!

Perhaps you're going too!
Who knows?
If you should get there first
Save just a little space for me
Close to the two I lost—
The smallest "Robe" will fit me
And just a bit of "Crown"—
For you know we do not mind our dress
When we are going home—

I'm glad I don't believe it
For it would stop my breath—
And I'd like to look a little more
At such a curious Earth!
I'm glad they did believe it
Whom I have never found
Since the mighty Autumn afternoon
I left them in the ground.

## 新的脚走在我的花园里

新的脚走在我的花园里——
新的手指拨动土地——
榆树上的吟游诗人
流露着孤独。

新的孩童在草地上玩耍——
新的疲倦者在地下长眠——
沉思的春天依旧回返——
白雪依旧如期而至！

**New feet within my garden go**

New feet within my garden go—
New fingers stir the sod—
A Troubadour upon the Elm
Betrays the solitude.

New children play upon the green—
New Weary sleep below—
And still the pensive Spring returns—
And still the punctual snow!

## 有一种科学，学者称其为

有一种科学，学者称其为，
"比较解剖学"——
它能让一根骨头——
揭示秘密，关于
某种罕见的生物腐烂消亡，
另一些朽化在岩石中——

富有远见的眼睛，
引我们去看
冬日草场上最温柔的花，
金黄的色彩
象征着各种玫瑰与百合，
还有千万只蝴蝶！

0100

## A science—so the Savants say

A science—so the Savants say,
"Comparative Anatomy"—
By which a single bone—
Is made a secret to unfold
Of some rare tenant of the mold,
Else perished in the stone—

So to the eye prospective led,
This meekest flower of the mead
Upon a winter's day,
Stands representative in gold
Of Rose and Lily, manifold,
And countless Butterfly!

0113

## 我们有一份黑夜需要忍耐

我们有一份黑夜需要忍耐——
我们有一份黎明——
我们缺失的极乐需要填满
我们缺失的轻蔑——

这里一颗星，那里一颗星，
还有几颗迷了路！
这里一片雾，那里一片雾，
之后，便是黎明！

0113

## Our share of night to bear

Our share of night to bear—
Our share of morning—
Our blank in bliss to fill
Our blank in scorning—

Here a star, and there a star,
Some lose their way!
Here a mist, and there a mist,
Afterwards—Day!

# 灵魂，你会再次投掷吗？

灵魂，你会再次投掷吗？
正是这样的骰子游戏
让数百人输掉，的确——
那几十人却赢得盆丰钵满——

天使令人屏息的投票
在此逗留记录你——
热切的精灵小组
为我的灵魂抽彩！

0139

**Soul, Wilt thou toss again?**

Soul, Wilt thou toss again?
By just such a hazard
Hundreds have lost indeed—
But tens have won an all—

Angel's breathless ballot
Lingers to record thee—
Imps in eager Caucus
Raffle for my Soul!

## 上帝保佑，他像战士一样离开

上帝保佑，他像战士一样离开，
火枪尚在胸膛——
上帝给他力量，冲锋陷阵
与最勇猛的对手搏斗！


上帝啊，请让我注视着他
白衣上镶着肩章——
我将不再惧怕敌人——
我将不再惧怕战斗！

0147

## Bless God, he went as soldiers

Bless God, he went as soldiers,
His musket on his breast—
Grant God, he charge the bravest
Of all the martial blest!

Please God, might I behold him
In epauletted white—
I should not fear the foe then—
I should not fear the fight!

## 尘土是唯一的秘密

尘土是唯一的秘密——
只有死亡
让你无法在他的"故乡"
找到全部真相。

没有人知道"他的父亲"——
他从不是一个孩子——
没有玩伴,
也没有"身世之谜"——

勤劳!寡言!
守时!庄重!
像匪徒般强硬!
比舰队更沉静!

他也像鸟儿一样筑巢!
却被上帝洗劫一空——
一只只知更鸟
被偷走,安息!

0153

**Dust is the only Secret**

Dust is the only Secret—
Death, the only One
You cannot find out all about
In his "native town."

Nobody knew "his Father"—
Never was a Boy—
Hadn't any playmates,
Or "Early history"—

Industrious! Laconic!
Punctual! Sedate!
Bold as a Brigand!
Stiller than a Fleet!

Builds, like a Bird, too!
Christ robs the Nest—
Robin after Robin
Smuggled to Rest!

## 0182

## 假如我不能活着

假如我不能活着
知更鸟飞来的时候，
请给那只穿红襟的，
一片面包屑作纪念。

假如我无法向你道谢，
只因在沉睡，
你要明白我正努力
张开花岗岩嘴唇！

0182

## If I shouldn't be alive

If I shouldn't be alive
When the Robins come,
Give the one in Red Cravat,
A Memorial crumb.

If I couldn't thank you,
Being fast asleep,
You will know I'm trying
With my Granite lip!

## "信仰"是一个精妙的发明

"信仰"是一个精妙的发明
对明眼的绅士来说——
若事出紧急
需谨慎使用显微镜。

0185

## "Faith" is a fine invention

"Faith" is a fine invention
When Gentlemen can see—
But Microscopes are prudent
In an Emergency.

## 0211

## 伊甸园，你慢慢地来！

伊甸园，你慢慢地来！
尚未习惯的嘴唇——
羞涩地靠向你，啜饮你的茉莉——
当虚弱的蜜蜂——


缓缓接近他的花朵，
围绕她的闺房哼唱——
清点他的花蜜——
进入，并沉醉在甘露中。

0211

**Come slowly—Eden!**

Come slowly—Eden!
Lips unused to Thee—
Bashful—sip thy Jessamines—
As the fainting Bee—

Reaching late his flower,
Round her chamber hums—
Counts his nectars—
Enters—and is lost in Balms.

## 我品尝未经酿造的酒

我品尝未经酿造的酒——
珍珠般的酒浆盛满大杯——
并非莱茵河畔所有的果子
都能制成这样的佳酿!

我是纵饮空气的酒鬼——
贪享露水的醉汉——
漫长的夏日——步履蹒跚——
跨出蓝至熔化的酒馆——

当"店主"将沉醉的蜜蜂
赶出吊钟花的大门——
当蝴蝶不再细细品酌——
我仍将痛饮几杯!

直到天使挥动雪白的礼帽——
圣徒们奔向窗口——
但见一个渺小的酒徒
斜倚着,太阳——

0214

# I taste a liquor never brewed

I taste a liquor never brewed—
From Tankards scooped in Pearl—
Not all the Vats upon the Rhine
Yield such an Alcohol!

Inebriate of Air—am I—
And Debauchee of Dew—
Reeling—thro endless summer days—
From inns of Molten Blue—

When "Landlords" turn the drunken Bee
Out of the Foxglove's door—
When Butterflies—renounce their "drams"—
I shall but drink the more!

Till Seraphs swing their snowy Hats—
And Saints—to windows run—
To see the little Tippler
Leaning against the—Sun—

## 什么是"天堂"

什么是"天堂"——
谁住在那里——
他们是"农民"吗——
需要"锄地"吗——
他们是否知道这里是"阿默斯特"——
是否知道,我也正在途中——

他们是否穿着"新鞋",在"伊甸园"——
那里是否存在永乐——
他们是否会责骂,每当我们想家
或是向上帝报告我们的乖戾——

你确信有那样一个人
形同"父亲",就在天上——
假如我在那里走失——
或者如护士所言,"死去"——
我也不用赤足,行走在"碧玉"上——
被救赎的人们,不会嘲笑我——
也许"伊甸园"并不像
昔日的新英格兰这般孤寂!

## What is—"Paradise"

What is—"Paradise"—
Who live there—
Are they "Farmers"—
Do they "hoe"—
Do they know that this is "Amherst"—
And that I—am coming—too—

Do they wear "new shoes"—in "Eden"—
Is it always pleasant—there—
Won't they scold us—when we're homesick—
Or tell God—how cross we are—

You are sure there's such a person
As "a Father"—in the sky—
So if I get lost—there—ever—
Or do what the Nurse calls "die"—
I shan't walk the "Jasper"—barefoot—
Ransomed folks—won't laugh at me—
Maybe—"Eden" a'n't so lonesome
As New England used to be!

## 0216

## 安然无恙地睡在玉室里

安然无恙地睡在玉室里——
温顺的复活者——
绸缎的椽木与石顶——
令他们无法感知——
清晨和正午——

新月之下，岁月一去不返——
行星在轨道上循环运转——
苍穹，昼夜更替——
王冠掉落，公爵臣服——
像无声的雪粒，落入盘中——

**0216**

## Safe in their Alabaster Chambers

Safe in their Alabaster Chambers—
Untouched by Morning—
And untouched by Noon—
Sleep the meek members of the Resurrection—
Rafter of Satin—and Roof of Stone!

Grand go the Years—in the Crescent—above
them—
Worlds scoop their Arcs—
And Firmaments—row—
Diadems—drop—and Doges—surrender—
Soundless as dots—On a Disk of Snow—

## 救世主！我无人可以倾诉

救世主！我无人可以倾诉——
只好来叨扰你。
正是我把你抛在脑后——
你是否还记得我？
我远道而来，并不为自己——
我没有什么分量——
我为你带来一颗威严的心
我无力承担——
我用自己的心将它负载——
直到我的心过于沉重——
奇怪，它越来越重——
是否太大，你无法接纳？

## Savior! I've no one else to tell

Savior! I've no one else to tell—
And so I trouble thee.
I am the one forgot thee so—
Dost thou remember me?
Nor, for myself, I came so far—
That were the little load—
I brought thee the imperial Heart
I had not strength to hold—
The Heart I carried in my own—
Till mine too heavy grew—
Yet—strangest—heavier since it went—
Is it too large for you?

## 今天，我是来买微笑的

今天，我是来买微笑的——
只要一个笑容——
你脸上最小的一个
就合乎我心意——
无人惦记的一个
那样微弱地闪现——
我在"柜台"恳求，先生——
您可卖得起——


我的手上，戴着钻石——
您可知道什么是钻石？
我有红宝石，像黑夜的鲜血——
还有黄宝石，璀璨如明星！
这真是犹太人的"交易"！
那么，我可否买下它，先生？

**0223**

**I Came to buy a smile—today**

I Came to buy a smile—today—
But just a single smile—
The smallest one upon your face
Will suit me just as well—
The one that no one else would miss
It shone so very small—
I'm pleading at the "counter"—sir—
Could you afford to sell—

I've Diamonds—on my fingers—
You know what Diamonds are?
I've Rubies—like the Evening Blood—
And Topaz—like the star!
'Twould be "a Bargain" for a Jew!
Say—may I have it—Sir?

## "天堂"，我难以触及！

"天堂"，我难以触及！
树上的苹果——
若是高高悬起，无从采摘——
便是，我的"天堂"！

流云上的色彩——
山后——
一片禁地，后面的房屋——
就是乐园的处所！

她嘲弄的紫袍，每个午后——
轻信的诱饵——
把魔术师深深恋慕——
就在昨天，我们遭到回绝！

0239

**"Heaven"—is what I cannot reach!**

"Heaven"—is what I cannot reach!
The Apple on the Tree—
Provided it do hopeless—hang—
That—"Heaven" is—to Me!

The Color, on the Cruising Cloud—
The interdicted Land—
Behind the Hill—the House behind—
There—Paradise—is found!

Her teasing Purples—Afternoons—
The credulous—decoy—
Enamored—of the Conjuror—
That spurned us—Yesterday!

## 我喜欢痛苦的表情

我喜欢痛苦的表情，
因为我知道它真实——
人们不会假作惊厥，
也不佯装，剧痛——

眼神一旦凝滞，就是死亡——
无法伪装额头上
由平凡的痛苦
串起的汗珠。

0241

## I like a look of Agony

I like a look of Agony,
Because I know it's true—
Men do not sham Convulsion,
Nor simulate, a Throe—

The Eyes glaze once—and that is Death—
Impossible to feign
The Beads upon the Forehead
By homely Anguish strung.

## 他们为何，把我关在天堂门外？

他们为何，把我关在天堂门外？
是不是，我的歌声太高？
但我能，放低"音调"
像鸟儿一般羞怯！

天使们是否愿意聆听我——
只不过，再多一次——
只不过，看看我是否会惊扰他们——
可别，把门关上！

哦，假如我，是那位先生
身穿"白袍"——
他们伸出小手，敲门——
我，会阻拦吗？

0248

## Why—do they shut Me out of Heaven?

Why—do they shut Me out of Heaven?
Did I sing—too loud?
But—I can say a little "Minor"
Timid as a Bird!

Wouldn't the Angels try me—
Just—once—more—
Just—see—if I troubled them—
But don't—shut the door!

Oh, if I—were the Gentleman
In the "White Robe"—
And they—were the little Hand—that
knocked—
Could—I—forbid?

## 暴风雨夜

暴风雨夜，暴风雨夜！
你若在我身边
狂风暴雨中
我们将共度春宵！

不惧狂风——
一颗泊进港湾的心——
丢掉罗盘——
丢掉海图！

划向伊甸园——
啊，大海！
今夜，我只想停泊——
在你深处！

0249

## Wild Nights—Wild Nights!

Wild Nights—Wild Nights!
Were I with thee
Wild Nights should be
Our luxury!

Futile—the Winds—
To a Heart in port—
Done with the Compass—
Done with the Chart!

Rowing in Eden—
Ah, the Sea!
Might I but moor—Tonight—
In Thee!

**0251**

## 篱笆那边

篱笆那边——
种着草莓——
篱笆那边——
我能翻过去，一试便知——
草莓多可口！

可是弄脏了围裙——
上帝一定会将我责怪！
哦，亲爱的，我猜，假如他是个孩子——
他也会翻过去，如果他可以！

0251

**Over the fence**

Over the fence—
Strawberries—grow—
Over the fence—
I could climb—if I tried, I know—
Berries are nice!

But—if I stained my Apron—
God would certainly scold!
Oh, dear,—I guess if He were a Boy—
He'd—climb—if He could!

0254

## "希望"长着翅膀

"希望"长着翅膀——
栖落在灵魂深处——
唱一曲无言的歌——
永不停歇,永不——

狂风中听见,悠扬的乐曲——
咆哮的风暴——
让这只小鸟进退两难
它温暖过许多人——

我曾听见它的歌,在最寒冷的地方——
在最偏僻的海上——
然而,身逢绝境,
它也不曾,向我索要一颗米粮。

0254

## "Hope" is the thing with feathers

"Hope" is the thing with feathers—
That perches in the soul—
And sings the tune without the words—
And never stops—at all—

And sweetest—in the Gale—is heard—
And sore must be the storm—
That could abash the little Bird
That kept so many warm—

I've heard it in the chillest land—
And on the strangest Sea—
Yet, never, in Extremity,
It asked a crumb—of Me.

## 在我脑海中，一场葬礼正在进行

在我脑海中，一场葬礼正在进行，
哀悼者来来回回
不停地踏步，踏步，直到
我的感觉被穿透——

当他们全体落座，
仪式开始，像鼓点——
不断地敲击，敲击，直到
我的意识逐渐麻木——

我听见人们抬起棺木——
从我的灵魂上嘎吱走过
仍旧穿着同样的，铅靴，
空间，响起钟鸣，

天堂仿佛化为丧钟，
存在，仅以耳朵听见，
我与寂静，形同异族
在此孤独，朽烂——

接着理性的木板，开始崩裂

我不断跌落，跌落——
每次下坠，都撞击着彼岸，
之后，失去所有知觉——

## I felt a Funeral, in my Brain

I felt a Funeral, in my Brain,
And Mourners to and fro
Kept treading—treading—till it seemed
That Sense was breaking through—

And when they all were seated,
A Service, like a Drum—
Kept beating—beating—till I thought
My Mind was going numb—

And then I heard them lift a Box
And creak across my Soul
With those same Boots of Lead, again,
Then Space—began to toll,

As all the Heavens were a Bell,
And Being, but an Ear,
And I, and Silence, some strange Race
Wrecked, solitary, here—

And then a Plank in Reason, broke,

And I dropped down, and down—
And hit a World, at every plunge,
And Finished knowing—then—

## 我是无名之辈！你是谁？

我是无名之辈！你是谁？
难道也一样，无足轻重？
我们刚好凑成一对，别声张！
有人会将我们驱逐，你知道！

做个大人物，多么悲哀！
抛头露面，像一只青蛙——
一天到晚，宣扬自己的姓名——
对着一片充满倾慕的泥潭！

**0288**

## I'm Nobody! Who are you?

I'm Nobody! Who are you?
Are you—Nobody—Too?
Then there's a pair of us?
Don't tell! they'd advertise—you know!

How dreary—to be—Somebody!
How public—like a Frog—
To tell one's name—the livelong June—
To an admiring Bog!

0292

## 假如你的勇气，将你否定

假如你的勇气，将你否定——
超越他吧——
假如他害怕调转方向，
他会紧靠墓碑——

那是个坚定的姿态——
绝不俯身屈就
手持黄铜武器——
最勇猛的巨人将它们锻造——

假如你的灵魂摇摆不定——
打开肉体之门吧——
怯懦者除了氧气——
别无他求——

0292

**If your Nerve, deny you**


If your Nerve, deny you—
Go above your Nerve—
He can lean against the Grave,
If he fear to swerve—

That's a steady posture—
Never any bend
Held of those Brass arms—
Best Giant made—

If your Soul seesaw—
Lift the Flesh door—
The Poltroon wants Oxygen—
Nothing more—

0301

## 我推想，大地是短暂的

我推想，大地是短暂的——
而苦痛，很绝对——
许多人受伤，
但，又将如何？


我推想，人终有一死——
最蓬勃的生机
亦无法免于腐朽，
但，又将如何？


我推想，在天堂——
会有，几分公平——
新的平等，被赋予——
但，又将如何？

0301

## I reason, Earth is short


I reason, Earth is short—
And Anguish—absolute—
And many hurt,
But, what of that?

I reason, we could die—
The best Vitality
Cannot excel Decay,
But, what of that?

I reason, that in Heaven—
Somehow, it will be even—
Some new Equation, given—
But, what of that?

## 像某种老式的奇迹

像某种老式的奇迹
当夏日时光远去——
夏天的回忆
和六月的趣事

像无尽的传说
像灰姑娘的栗色马——
或是绿林英雄，小约翰——
蓝胡子的陈列室——

她的蜜蜂发出虚构的嗡鸣——
她的花朵，仿佛梦境——
几乎令我们，喜极而泣——
它们看上去，如此真切——

她的回忆似旋律，重现——
当乐队喑哑无声——
小提琴放回琴盒——
耳朵，与天堂，失去知觉——

0302

## Like Some Old fashioned Miracle

Like Some Old fashioned Miracle
When Summertime is done—
Seems Summer's Recollection
And the Affairs of June

As infinite Tradition
As Cinderella's Bays—
Or Little John—of Lincoln Green—
Or Blue Beard's Galleries—

Her Bees have a fictitious Hum—
Her Blossoms, like a Dream—
Elate us—till we almost weep—
So plausible—they seem—

Her Memories like Strains—Review—
When Orchestra is dumb—
The Violin in Baize replaced—
And Ear—and Heaven—numb—

0303

## 灵魂选择她自己的侣伴

灵魂选择她自己的侣伴——
然后，关上门——
忠于内心神圣的选择——
不再抛头露面——

不为所动，她看见车辇，停在——
她低矮的门前——
不为所动，即使君王拜倒在
她的石榴裙边——

我了解她，于茫茫人海中——
选择了唯一——
从此心无杂念——
坚如磐石——

0303

## The Soul selects her own Society

The Soul selects her own Society—
Then—shuts the Door—
To her divine Majority—
Present no more—

Unmoved—she notes the Chariots—pausing—
At her low Gate—
Unmoved—an Emperor be kneeling
Upon her Mat—

I've known her—from an ample nation—
Choose One—
Then—close the Valves of her attention—
Like Stone—

**0305**

## 绝望不同于

绝望不同于
恐惧，就像车船
失事的瞬间——
与一具残骸的差别——

平和的思想，安宁——
满足，犹如塑像
额前的双眼——
它明白，眼睛看不见——

0305

## The difference between Despair

The difference between Despair
And Fear—is like the One
Between the instant of a Wreck—
And when the Wreck has been—

The Mind is smooth—no Motion—
Contented as the Eye
Upon the Forehead of a Bust—
That knows—it cannot see—

## 我送走两个日落

我送走两个日落——
我和白天赛跑——
我送走两个，还有星星几颗——
而他，只送出一个——

他的更宽阔，而正如
我对一个朋友所说——
我的那个，小巧可爱
一双手就可携带——

0308

**I send Two Sunsets**

I send Two Sunsets—
Day and I—in competition ran—
I finished Two—and several Stars—
While He—was making One—

His own was ampler—but as I
Was saying to a friend—
Mine—is the more convenient
To Carry in the Hand—

## 他摸索你的灵魂

他摸索你的灵魂

像乐师抚摸琴键

然后奏响完整的乐章——

他逐渐让你惊叹——

为你脆弱的天性做好防备

迎接超凡的一击

以音槌轻轻击打——

由远及近，徐徐而来

等你的呼吸得到平复——

头脑慢慢冷静——

再向你施以威严的霹雳——

把你裸露的灵魂剥去外皮——

当风的巨手摇撼森林——

宇宙寂然无声——

**0315**

**He fumbles at your Soul**

He fumbles at your Soul
As Players at the Keys
Before they drop full Music on—
He stuns you by degrees—
Prepares your brittle Nature
For the Ethereal Blow
By fainter Hammers—further heard—
Then nearer—Then so slow
Your Breath has time to straighten—
Your Brain—to bubble Cool—
Deals—One—imperial—Thunderbolt—
That scalps your naked Soul—

When Winds take Forests in their Paws—
The Universe—is still—

## 有些人守安息日去教堂

有些人守安息日去教堂——
而我，在家里守——
用一只长刺歌雀唱诗——
果园，就是穹顶——


有些人守安息日身穿白袍——
而我只佩戴翅膀——
没有教堂的，鸣钟，
我们的小司事——歌唱。


上帝传道，他是知名的牧师——
这诫训从来不长久，
我最终，没有去天堂——
我一直在，行路。

0324

## Some keep the Sabbath going to Church

Some keep the Sabbath going to Church—
I keep it, staying at Home—
With a Bobolink for a Chorister—
And an Orchard, for a Dome—

Some keep the Sabbath in Surplice—
I just wear my Wings—
And instead of tolling the Bell, for Church,
Our little Sexton—sings.

God preaches, a noted Clergyman—
And the sermon is never long,
So instead of getting to Heaven, at last—
I'm going, all along.

## 在我的一只眼失明前

在我的一只眼失明前
我愿意去看——
像其他拥有双眼的生灵一样
我知道别无他法——


假如今天，有人说——
我可以拥有
天空，我会告诉你我的心
将因此裂开，我无法容纳——


草场，属于我——
群山，属于我——
万林，浩瀚的星河——
正午的景象，我尽可取拿
以我有限的视野——


翻飞腾跃的小鸟——
清晨琥珀色的小路——
属于我，任凭我喜爱时去看——
多看一眼将令我死去——

更安全的方式，我猜想，是将灵魂

置于窗台之上——

那里存放着生灵的眼睛——

对阳光毫无戒心——

0327

**Before I got my eye put out**

Before I got my eye put out
I liked as well to see—
As other Creatures, that have Eyes
And know no other way—

But were it told to me—Today—
That I might have the sky
For mine—I tell you that my Heart
Would split, for size of me—

The Meadows—mine—
The Mountains—mine—
All Forests—Stintless Stars—
As much of Noon as I could take
Between my finite eyes—

The Motions of the Dipping Birds—
The Morning's Amber Road—
For mine—to look at when I liked—
The News would strike me dead—

So safer—guess—with just my soul

Upon the Window pane—

Where other Creatures put their eyes—

Incautious—of the Sun—

0328

## 一只鸟，飞落在小路上

一只鸟，飞落在小路上——
并不知道我在一旁——
看它将一只虫子啄成两半
再生吞下肚，

接着，它在近旁的草叶上
啜饮一滴露水——
又轻跃到墙边
给一只甲虫让路——

它飞快地转转眼珠
茫然环顾四周——
像两颗惊恐的珠子，我这样想——
它晃着丝绒般的小脑袋

仿佛身处危险，小心翼翼，
我丢给它一块面包屑
它便舒展羽毛
拍拍翅膀飞回了家——

比船桨拨开海水更温柔，

银色的海面没有波澜——
比正午飞离沙洲的蝴蝶更轻盈
不溅起一朵浪花。

0328

## A Bird came down the Walk

A Bird came down the Walk—
He did not know I saw—
He bit an Angleworm in halves
And ate the fellow, raw,

And then he drank a Dew
From a convenient Grass—
And then hopped sidewise to the Wall
To let a Beetle pass—

He glanced with rapid eyes
That hurried all around—
They looked like frightened Beads, I thought—
He stirred his Velvet Head

Like one in danger, Cautious,
I offered him a Crumb
And he unrolled his feathers
And rowed him softer home—

Than Oars divide the Ocean,

Too silver for a seam—
Or Butterflies, off Banks of Noon
Leap, plashless as they swim.

0333
## 小草无事可做

小草无事可做——
一片朴素的绿色——
只能育养几只蝴蝶
款待几只蜜蜂——

它整日伴着和风
美妙的曲调摇曳——
把阳光抱在膝头
向万物鞠躬行礼——

它彻夜把露滴串成珠链——
悉心装扮自己
容貌如此出众
令公爵夫人黯然失色——

即使它死去，也将带着——
神圣的气味消逝——
像卑微的香料，长眠
像香松，枯萎——

然后，住进尊贵的谷仓——

把岁月虚度，

小草无事可做

我愿成为干草一株——

0333

## The Grass so little has to do

The Grass so little has to do—
A Sphere of simple Green—
With only Butterflies to brood
And Bees to entertain—

And stir all day to pretty Tunes
The Breezes fetch along—
And hold the Sunshine in its lap
And bow to everything—

And thread the Dews, all night, like
Pearls—
And make itself so fine
A Duchess were too common
For such a noticing—

And even when it dies—to pass—
In Odors so divine—
Like Lowly spices, lain to sleep
Or Spikenards, perishing—

And then, in Sovereign Barns to dwell—
And dream the Days away,
The Grass so little has to do
I wish I were a Hay—

0361

## 我能做到的，我情愿

我能做到的，我情愿——
尽管它像水仙微不足道——
我做不到的，必定
还无从知晓——

## What I can do—I will

What I can do—I will—
Though it be little as a Daffodil—
That I cannot—must be
Unknown to possibility—

0363

## 我去向她致谢

我去向她致谢——
但她已睡去——
她的床，一块狭窄的石头——
头与脚放满——
访客们携来的花——

谁去向她致谢——
但她已睡去——
漂洋过海，将她探望——
仿佛她尚在人世，这过程虽短——
但归途，却很漫长——

0363

**I went to thank Her**

I went to thank Her—
But She Slept—
Her Bed—a funneled Stone—
With Nosegays at the Head and Foot—
That Travellers—had thrown—

Who went to thank Her—
But She Slept—
'Twas Short—to cross the Sea—
To look upon Her like—alive—
But turning back—'twas slow—

**0374**

## 我去过天堂

我去过天堂——
那是一座红宝石——
点亮的小镇——
铺满羽绒——

它寂静，胜过
落满露珠的田野——
像浑然天成的——
美丽画卷。
居民，像精美花边——
制成的飞蛾——
职责，轻如薄纱——
姓名，柔似绒毛——
置身如此珍奇的——
情境中——
我几乎——
感到心满意足——

0374

## I went to Heaven

I went to Heaven—
'Twas a small Town—
Lit—with a Ruby—
Lathed—with Down—

Stiller—than the fields
At the full Dew—
Beautiful—as Pictures—
No Man drew.
People—like the Moth—
Of Mechlin—frames—
Duties—of Gossamer—
And Eider—names—
Almost—contented—
I—could be—
'Mong such unique
Society—

## 我当然祈祷过

我当然祈祷过——
可上帝在乎吗？
在他眼中这不过是
空中的鸟，跺了跺脚——
大喊着"给我"——
生存的理由——
我不曾有过，若不是因为你——
将我留在原子的坟墓里——
快乐，虚无，欢愉，麻木——
比起这锥心的痛苦
已是一种仁慈。

## Of Course—I prayed

Of Course—I prayed—

And did God Care?

He cared as much as on the Air

A Bird—had stamped her foot—

And cried "Give Me"—

My Reason—Life—

I had not had—but for Yourself—

'Twere better Charity

To leave me in the Atom's Tomb—

Merry, and Nought, and gay, and numb—

Than this smart Misery.

**0378**

## 我看不见路，天堂被缝起

我看不见路，天堂被缝起——
我感到门柱在闭合——
地球颠倒了两极——
我触摸宇宙——

它接着向后滑，我独自一人——
如球体上的斑点——
在圆周上行走——
听不见半点钟声——

0378

**I saw no Way—The Heavens were stitched**

I saw no Way—The Heavens were stitched—
I felt the Columns close—
The Earth reversed her Hemispheres—
I touched the Universe—

And back it slid—and I alone—
A Speck upon a Ball—
Went out upon Circumference—
Beyond the Dip of Bell—

## 秘密一旦说出

秘密一旦说出——
就不再是秘密，那么——
秘密，若被保守——
则令人惊骇——

保持对秘密的畏惧——
好过——
对旁人，道破——

0381

## A Secret told

A Secret told—
Ceases to be a Secret—then—
A Secret—kept—
That—can appal but One—

Better of it—continual be afraid—
Than it—
And Whom you told it to—beside—

0384

## 没有酷刑能折磨我

没有酷刑能折磨我——
我的灵魂，是自由的——
这终将朽烂的骨架背后
正编织着更无畏的一种——


铁锯无法将它凿破——
弯刀也不能将它刺穿——
就这样，两副身躯——
一个被缚束，另一个飞走——


苍鹰并不像你
能轻易放弃——
它的巢穴
收获整个天空——


除非你
与自己为敌——
是被奴役，还是自由——
全在于你的觉悟。

0384

## No Rack can torture me

No Rack can torture me—
My Soul—at Liberty—
Behind this mortal Bone
There knits a bolder One—

You cannot prick with saw—
Nor pierce with Scimitar—
Two Bodies—therefore be—
Bind One—The Other fly—

The Eagle of his Nest
No easier divest—
And gain the Sky
Than mayest Thou—

Except Thyself may be
Thine Enemy—
Captivity is Consciousness—
So's Liberty.

# 请回答我，七月

请回答我，七月——
蜜蜂在哪儿——
干草在哪儿——
羞红的脸颊在哪儿？

啊，七月说——
种子在哪儿——
蓓蕾在哪儿——
五月花在哪儿——
请你回答我——

不，五月花说——
让我看看雪花——
让我听听铃声——
让我看看松鸦！

松鸦叫个不停——
玉米在哪儿——
薄雾在哪儿——
刺果在哪儿？
岁末说，在这里——

0386

**Answer July**

Answer July—
Where is the Bee—
Where is the Blush—
Where is the Hay?

Ah, said July—
Where is the Seed—
Where is the Bud—
Where is the May—
Answer Thee—Me—

Nay—said the May—
Show me the Snow—
Show me the Bells—
Show me the Jay!

Quibbled the Jay—
Where be the Maize—
Where be the Haze—
Where be the Bur?
Here—said the Year—

## 最甜美的异端邪说认为

最甜美的异端邪说认为
男人和女人都了解——
彼此的信仰——
尽管这种信仰只接纳两个人——

礼拜进行得这样频繁——
仪式，这样琐碎——
恩赐是这样必不可免——
背弃，即为不忠——

0387

**The Sweetest Heresy received**

The Sweetest Heresy received

That Man and Woman know—

Each Other's Convert—

Though the Faith accommodate but Two—


The Churches are so frequent—

The Ritual—so small—

The Grace so unavoidable—

To fail—is Infidel—

0392

## 穿透黑暗的泥土，像经受教育

穿透黑暗的泥土，像经受教育——
百合花定会通过——
她洁白的脚，毫不颤抖——
她的信仰，无所畏惧——


从此以后，在草地上——
她晃动绿玉的铃铛——
霉腐的日子，此刻尽已遗忘——
喜不自禁，在林中谷地——

0392

## Through the Dark Sod—as Education

Through the Dark Sod—as Education—
The Lily passes sure—
Feels her white foot—no trepidation—
Her faith—no fear—

Afterward—in the Meadow—
Swinging her Beryl Bell—
The Mold—life—all forgotten—now—
In Ecstasy—and Dell—

## 那是爱，不是我

那是爱，不是我——
哦，去责罚，我恳请——
那真正为你而死的——
是他，不是我——


爱你，胜于一切，此罪！
也重于一切——
最不应被赦免——
像耶稣一样，至深！


请法官不要弄错——
我们俩这样相像——
但身负重罪的——
是爱，现在，动手！

0394

**'Twas Love—not me**

'Twas Love—not me—
Oh punish—pray—
The Real one died for Thee—
Just Him—not me—

Such Guilt—to love Thee—most!
Doom it beyond the Rest—
Forgive it—last—
'Twas base as Jesus—most!

Let Justice not mistake—
We Two—looked so alike—
Which was the Guilty Sake—
'Twas Love's—Now Strike!

这是我写给世界的信

## 当钻石是一个传说

当钻石是一个传说，
王冠，一个故事——
我独自种下胸针和耳环，
成熟之日，将它们卖掉——


尽管无人问津，与世无争，
我的艺术，在一个夏日，拥有守护神——
它曾是一位王后——
它曾是一只蝴蝶——

0397

## When Diamonds are a Legend

When Diamonds are a Legend,
And Diadems—a Tale—
I Brooch and Earrings for Myself,
Do sow, and Raise for sale—

And tho' I'm scarce accounted,
My Art, a Summer Day—had Patrons—
Once—it was a Queen—
And once—a Butterfly—

**0423**

## 月有始末，年，是一个结

月有始末，年，是一个结——
没有什么力量能解开
一团苦难
让它略为伸展——


大地将倦怠的生命
收入她神秘的抽屉——
如此温柔，勿须怀疑
它们已陷入长眠——


疲惫了一整天的——
孩子们的举止——
他们自己，是喧哗的玩具
无法妥善收存——

0423

**The Months have ends—the Years—a knot**

The Months have ends—the Years—a knot—
No Power can untie
To stretch a little further
A Skein of Misery—

The Earth lays back these tired lives
In her mysterious Drawers—
Too tenderly, that any doubt
An ultimate Repose—

The manner of the Children—
Who weary of the Day—
Themself—the noisy Plaything
They cannot put away—

## 早安，午夜

早安，午夜——
我要回家了——
白天，厌倦了我——
我怎能对他厌倦？

阳光照耀的地方很美——
我喜欢在那里逗留——
但现在早晨，不要我了——
所以晚安，白天！

我还能看一看，对吗？
当东方红霞满天——
山岭总有办法，在那时——
让心畅游四方——

你并不那样美，午夜——
我选择了白天——
但是，请接受一个小女孩吧——
他却转过身去！

**0425**

## Good Morning—Midnight

Good Morning—Midnight—
I'm coming Home—
Day—got tired of Me—
How could I—of Him?

Sunshine was a sweet place—
I liked to stay—
But Morn—didn't want me—now—
So—Goodnight—Day!

I can look—can't I—
When the East is Red?
The Hills—have a way—then—
That puts the Heart—abroad—

You—are not so fair—Midnight—
I chose—Day—
But—please take a little Girl—
He turned away!

## 月亮离海很远

月亮离海很远——
但她琥珀色的手——
引领着他，像一个温驯的男孩——
涌向海岸——

他从不失分寸——
在她的目光下变得顺从
他的浪花只到这里，向着城镇的方向——
只到这里，便又消退——

哦，先生，你那，琥珀色的手——
还有我的，遥远的海——
你任何一个目光的授意
都将令我唯命是从——

0429

**The Moon is distant from the Sea**

The Moon is distant from the Sea—
And yet, with Amber Hands—
She leads Him—docile as a Boy—
Along appointed Sands—

He never misses a Degree—
Obedient to Her Eye
He comes just so far—toward the Town—
Just so far—goes away—

Oh, Signor, Thine, the Amber Hand—
And mine—the distant Sea—
Obedient to the least command
Thine eye impose on me—

## 埋进坟墓的人们

埋进坟墓的人们，
都会朽烂吗？
我确信一个物种
还像我一样

活着，我能证明
我否认我已死去——
用头顶上方的，储气罐——
充满肺部，以此见证——

耶稣曾说，让我告诉你——
有一种人存在——
他们永远尝不到死的滋味——
假如耶稣诚恳的话——

我无须再做争辩——
上帝的话
不容置疑——
他告诉我，死亡已死——

0432

## Do People moulder equally

Do People moulder equally,
They bury, in the Grave?
I do believe a Species
As positively live

As I, who testify it
Deny that I—am dead—
And fill my Lungs, for Witness—
From Tanks—above my Head—

I say to you, said Jesus—
That there be standing here—
A Sort, that shall not taste of Death—
If Jesus was sincere—

I need no further Argue—
That statement of the Lord
Is not a controvertible—
He told me, Death was dead—

## 知道如何忘记！

知道如何忘记！
但能否授之于人？
最简单的艺术，人们说
只要懂得方法

愚钝的心
因求知而死
为科学牺牲
已是寻常，但如今——

我去念书
也并未变得聪慧
地球仪不能讲解
对数也无法传授

"如何忘记"！
请哲学家来说！
啊，非博学
不能掌握！

它写在书里吗？

那样，我可以买回——
它的样子像行星吗？
望远镜了解——

假如它是发明
必须拥有专利。
智慧书的教士
你怎会不知？

0433

**Knows how to forget!**

Knows how to forget!
But could It teach it?
Easiest of Arts, they say
When one learn how

Dull Hearts have died
In the Acquisition
Sacrifice for Science
Is common, though, now—

I went to School
But was not wiser
Globe did not teach it
Nor Logarithm Show

"How to forget"!
Say—some—Philosopher!
Ah, to be erudite
Enough to know!

Is it in a Book?

So, I could buy it—
Is it like a Planet?
Telescopes would know—

If it be invention
It must have a Patent.
Rabbi of the Wise Book
Don't you know?

## 过于疯狂是至高的理性

过于疯狂是至高的理性——
对明眼人而言——
过于理性，是纯粹的疯狂——
大多数人，对此
人云亦云——
你若赞同，就是理性之人——
稍有异议，就是危险分子——
需以锁链加身——

## Much Madness is divinest Sense

Much Madness is divinest Sense—
To a discerning Eye—
Much Sense—the starkest Madness—
'Tis the Majority
In this, as All, prevail—
Assent—and you are sane—
Demur—you're straightway dangerous—
And handled with a Chain—

## 濒临饥亡的人把高度意义

濒临饥亡的人把高度意义
赋予食物——
遥不可及,他叹息,因此
绝望——
也因此美好——


只要进食,就能解饿,千真万确——
但也证实
一经获得
佳肴飞走,鲜美可口的——
是距离——

0439

## Undue Significance a starving man attaches

Undue Significance a starving man attaches
To Food—
Far off—He sighs—and therefore—Hopeless—
And therefore—Good—

Partaken—it relieves—indeed—
But proves us
That Spices fly
In the Receipt—It was the Distance—
Was Savory—

**0440**

## 我们习惯在离别时

我们习惯在离别时
赠予对方小饰物——
它助我们坚定信念
当有情人天各一方——


人的喜好相异，礼物各有不同——
铁线莲，临行之前——
送给我一缕
她卷曲的电发——

**0440**

## 'Tis customary as we part

'Tis customary as we part
A trinket—to confer—
It helps to stimulate the faith
When Lovers be afar—

'Tis various—as the various taste—
Clematis—journeying far—
Presents me with a single Curl
Of her Electric Hair—

## 这是我写给世界的信

这是我写给世界的信
她却从未给我回信——
大自然告诉我最简单的消息——
以温柔的庄严

我将她的讯息
交托于一双无形的手——
为了她所爱的，亲切的同胞——
请将我，宽容地评判

**0441**

## This is my letter to the World

This is my letter to the World
That never wrote to Me—
The simple News that Nature told—
With tender Majesty

Her Message is committed
To Hands I cannot see—
For love of Her—Sweet—countrymen—
Judge tenderly—of Me

**0442**

## 上帝造了一棵小龙胆草

上帝造了一棵小龙胆草——
她想努力变成一朵玫瑰——
却失败了，夏天将她取笑——
可就在冬雪降临前


那里长出了一个紫色的花苞——
群山为之倾倒——
夏天遮住自己的额头——
嘲笑，变为沉默——


在严寒中，她亭亭玉立——
提尔紫不会出现
只等北风将她催开——
主啊，我可以绽放吗？

## God made a little Gentian

God made a little Gentian—
It tried—to be a Rose—
And failed—and all the Summer laughed—
But just before the Snows

There rose a Purple Creature—
That ravished all the Hill—
And Summer hid her Forehead—
And Mockery—was still—

The Frosts were her condition—
The Tyrian would not come
Until the North—invoke it—
Creator—Shall I—bloom?

## 活着令人感到羞耻

活着令人感到羞耻——
如此英勇的人，已经死去——
有人羡慕高贵的尘土——
将这样的头颅掩埋——


石碑告诉世人，斯巴达勇士
为谁战死
我们并未拥有，他所拥有的品行
去换取自由——


代价昂贵，我们庄严付出——
一种像堆叠钞票一样
堆叠生命，才能获取的东西——
我们可配得到？


在等待中，我们的价值是否大到——
足以让生命这颗硕大的珍珠
因自己消融于——
战争可怕的酒杯中？


活着，也许是荣誉——

我想，那些逝者——

那些阵亡的将士，是救世主——

彰显出神圣——

**0444**

**It feels a shame to be Alive**

It feels a shame to be Alive—
When Men so brave—are dead—
One envies the Distinguished Dust—
Permitted—such a Head—

The Stone—that tells defending Whom
This Spartan put away
What little of Him we—possessed
In Pawn for Liberty—

The price is great—Sublimely paid—
Do we deserve—a Thing—
That lives—like Dollars—must be piled
Before we may obtain?

Are we that wait—sufficient worth—
That such Enormous Pearl
As life—dissolved be—for Us—
In Battle's—horrid Bowl?

It may be—a Renown to live—

I think the Men who die—

Those unsustained—Saviors—

Present Divinity—

**0447**

## 我能，多做些什么，为你

我能，多做些什么，为你——
假如你是一只黄蜂——
既然我，能敬献蜂王的——
唯有一束花？

0447

## Could—I do more—for Thee

Could—I do more—for Thee—
Wert Thou a Bumble Bee—
Since for the Queen, have I—
Nought but Bouquet?

## 这就是诗人，是他

这就是诗人，是他
从寻常意义中
提炼不凡之道——
从凋零在门前

惯见的落花中
炼制精纯的玫瑰油——
令我们惊愕
并非我们先来获得——

一幅幅图景，诗人——
是他，为我们铺展——
使我们与之相较——
身处无尽的贫穷——

他的所有，不知不觉——
被夺走少许，却无损害——
他是他自己的财富——
超越时光——

**0448**

## This was a Poet—It is That

This was a Poet—It is That
Distills amazing sense
From ordinary Meanings—
And Attar so immense

From the familiar species
That perished by the Door—
We wonder it was not Ourselves
Arrested it—before—

Of Pictures, the Discloser—
The Poet—it is He—
Entitles Us—by Contrast—
To ceaseless Poverty—

Of portion—so unconscious—
The Robbing—could not harm—
Himself—to Him—a Fortune—
Exterior—to Time—

## 我为美而死

我为美而死，却还不能
适应坟墓
一个为真理而死的人
正躺在我的隔壁——

他轻声地问，"你为何而死？"
"为了美。"我回答——
"我，为真理，它们本是一体——
我们，是同胞。"他说——

就这样，像亲人，重逢在夜里——
我们隔墙而谈——
直到青苔爬上我们的嘴唇——
覆盖我们的姓名——

0449

# I died for Beauty

I died for Beauty—but was scarce
Adjusted in the Tomb
When One who died for Truth, was lain
In an adjoining Room—

He questioned softly "Why I failed"?
"For Beauty", I replied—
"And I—for Truth—Themself are One—
We Brethren, are", He said—

And so, as Kinsmen, met a Night—
We talked between the Rooms—
Until the Moss had reached our lips—
And covered up—our names—

## 梦，真好，醒来更好

梦，真好，醒来更好，
假如醒在清晨——
假如醒在午夜，更好——
梦想着破晓时分——

疑惑的知更鸟，阴郁的树——
远远好过——
一个凝固的黎明，对抗着——
永不抵达的光明——

0450

**Dreams—are well—but Waking's better**

Dreams—are well—but Waking's better,
If One wake at Morn—
If One wake at Midnight—better—
Dreaming—of the Dawn—

Sweeter—the Surmising Robins—
Never gladdened Tree—
Than a Solid Dawn—confronting—
Leading to no Day—

## 诸神将它赐予我

诸神将它赐予我——
在我年幼时——
他们总在我们还幼小、稚嫩的时候——
送来最多礼物，你知道。
我将它置于掌心——
从不放下——
不敢吃，也不敢睡——
生怕它不翼而飞——
当我匆匆赶往学校——
我听见"富有"这样的词——
来自街角的某些嘴唇——
我勉强挤出微笑。
富有！这正是我，我富有——
以黄金之名——
我拥有的，仿佛是根根金条——
这种差别，让我无畏——

## It was given to me by the Gods

It was given to me by the Gods—
When I was a little Girl—
They given us Presents most—you know—
When we are new—and small.
I kept it in my Hand—
I never put it down—
I did not dare to eat—or sleep—
For fear it would be gone—
I heard such words as "Rich"—
When hurrying to school—
From lips at Corners of the Streets—
And wrestled with a smile.
Rich! 'Twas Myself—was rich—
To take the name of Gold—
And Gold to own—in solid Bars—
The Difference—made me bold—

## 临死之前，我听见苍蝇的嗡叫

临死之前，我听见苍蝇的嗡叫——
房间里的沉静
像风暴将至——
空气中的死寂——

人们的双眼，泪已流干——
呼吸变得紧促
最后到来的一刻，当死神
降临这间屋子——

我将身外之物，放进遗愿
给予人们我能给予的
一切就在那时
一只苍蝇乘虚飞入——

蓝色，微弱，起伏的嗡叫——
在光与我之间——
接着窗帘突然被阖上，于是
我再也无法看见——

**0465**

**I heard a Fly buzz—when I died**

I heard a Fly buzz—when I died—
The Stillness in the Room
Was like the Stillness in the Air—
Between the Heaves of Storm—

The Eyes around—had wrung them dry—
And Breaths were gathering firm
For that last Onset—when the King
Be witnessed—in the Room—

I willed my Keepsakes—Signed away
What portions of me be
Assignable—and then it was
There interposed a Fly—

With Blue—uncertain stumbling Buzz—
Between the light—and me—
And then the Windows failed—and then
I could not see to see—

## 我们不在坟边玩耍

我们不在坟边玩耍——
那里地方不大——
况且地面不平、倾斜
前来探访的人们——

在墓碑上放一朵花——
并垂下脸庞——
我们生怕，他们的心也坠落——
砸碎我们快乐的游戏——

因此我们搬到远方
如同躲避敌人——
只是偶尔四下看看
距离，有多远——

0467

## We do not play on Graves

We do not play on Graves—
Because there isn't Room—
Besides—it isn't even—it slants
And People come—

And put a Flower on it—
And hang their faces so—
We're fearing that their Hearts will drop—
And crush our pretty play—

And so we move as far
As Enemies—away—
Just looking round to see how far
It is—Occasionally—

## 火红的，光芒，是黎明

火红的，光芒，是黎明——
紫罗兰色，是正午——
黄色，是白昼，渐渐流逝——
所有色彩，随之消隐——


然而夜晚，星辉闪耀——
照亮这片曾经燃烧过的广阔——
这银白的疆土
永不会燃尽——

**0469**

## The Red—Blaze—is the Morning

The Red—Blaze—is the Morning—
The Violet—is Noon—
The Yellow—Day—is falling—
And after that—is none—

But Miles of Sparks—at Evening—
Reveal the Width that burned—
The Territory Argent—that
Never yet—consumed—

## 我没有时间去恨

我没有时间去恨——
因为
坟墓会阻止我——
生命并未
充裕到
令我去恨的地步——

我也没有时间去爱——
但是既然
生活难免操劳——
以微薄的力量去爱——
我想
对我来说已足够艰辛——

0478

## I had no time to Hate

I had no time to Hate—
Because
The Grave would hinder Me—
And Life was not so
Ample I
Could finish—Enmity—

Nor had I time to Love—
But since
Some Industry must be—
The little Toil of Love—
I thought
Be large enough for Me—

## "我为什么爱"你，先生？

"我为什么爱"你，先生？
因为——
风不祈求青草
回答，他经过时
她为何摇摆不定。

他知道，而你
却不知——
我们并未——
足够了解
顺其自然的智慧——

闪电，从不问眼睛
他经过时，它为何闭上——
他知道眼睛不说话——
言语无法——
道尽缘由——
睿智的人们，心领神会——

日出，先生，我无法抗拒——

因为他是日出，我看见——

于是就这样——

我爱你——

0480

## "Why do I love" You, Sir?

"Why do I love" You, Sir?
Because—
The Wind does not require the Grass
To answer—Wherefore when He pass
She cannot keep Her place.

Because He knows—and
Do not You—
And We know not—
Enough for Us
The Wisdom it be so—

The Lightning—never asked an Eye
Wherefore it shut—when He was by—
Because He knows it cannot speak—
And reasons not contained—
—Of Talk—
There be—preferred by Daintier Folk—

The Sunrise—Sir—compelleth Me—

Because He's Sunrise—and I see—

Therefore—Then—

I love Thee—

## 假如你在秋天到来

假如你在秋天到来，
我会轻掠过夏天
一半轻笑，一半轻蔑，
像主妇们轻轻掸去一只苍蝇。

假如一年之中我能见到你，
我会将每个月缠绕成球——
放进不同的抽屉，
不愿它们再融为一体——

假如还要几个世纪，那样长久，
我会用双手细数，
逐日递减，直到我的手指
坠入塔斯马尼亚的岛屿。

假如命由天定，我们各自——
要过完今生，才能相见
我会像扔掉果壳一样，扔掉它，
就此走向永恒——

然而现在，你我之间

等待的长短，未知，
它蜇了我，像一只顽皮的蜜蜂——
我却无法诉说，这种刺痛。

**If you were coming in the Fall**

If you were coming in the Fall,
I'd brush the Summer by
With half a smile, and half a spurn,
As Housewives do, a Fly.

If I could see you in a year,
I'd wind the months in balls—
And put them each in separate Drawers,
For fear the numbers fuse—

If only Centuries, delayed,
I'd count them on my Hand,
Subtracting, till my fingers dropped
Into Van Dieman's Land.

If certain, when this life was out—
That yours and mine, should be
I'd toss it yonder, like a Rind,
And take Eternity—

But, now, uncertain of the length

Of this, that is between,
It goads me, like the Goblin Bee—
That will not state—its sting.

## 美，不经雕琢，与生俱来

美，不经雕琢，与生俱来——
若去追逐，它必闪躲——
顺其自然，它将永驻——


超越时光


牧场上，当风的手指
轻抚过草地——
神赐予的美
你永远无法造就——

0516

**Beauty—be not caused—It Is**

Beauty—be not caused—It Is—
Chase it, and it ceases—
Chase it not, and it abides—

Overtake the Creases

In the Meadow—when the Wind
Runs his fingers thro' it—
Deity will see to it
That You never do it—

## 离别，去接受审判

离别，去接受审判——
庄严的午后——
壮阔的云，像接待员，聚集——
万物冷眼旁观——

肉身，交出，消除——
无形之物，诞生——
两个世界，像观众各自散去——
徒剩灵魂，孤独——

0524

**Departed—to the Judgment**

Departed—to the Judgment—
A Mighty—Afternoon—
Great Clouds—like Ushers—leaning—
Creation—looking on—

The Flesh—Surrendered—Cancelled—
The Bodiless—begun—
Two Worlds—like Audiences—disperse—
And leave the Soul—alone—

## 你无法扑灭一种火

你无法扑灭一种火——
它点燃自己
兀自蔓延，不需扇风——
在这漫漫长夜——

你无法收起一场洪水——
将它关进抽屉——
因为风会找到它——
再告诉你的松木地板——

0530

**You cannot put a Fire out**

You cannot put a Fire out—
A Thing that can ignite
Can go, itself, without a Fan—
Upon the slowest Night—

You cannot fold a Flood—
And put it in a Drawer—
Because the Winds would find it out—
And tell your Cedar Floor—

## 我手持自己的力量

我手持自己的力量——
去对抗世界——
我的力量远不及大卫[1]——
但我，有双倍的胆识——

我以卵石瞄准，但我自己
却是唯一倒下的人——
是因为歌利亚[2]太高大——
还是我自己，太渺小？

---

1　大卫（David），即大卫王，以色列王国国王。

2　歌利亚（Goliath），传说中的著名巨人之一。《圣经》记载，歌利亚是非利士将军，带兵进攻以色列军队，他拥有无穷的力量。大卫用投石弹弓打中歌利亚的脑袋，并割下他的首级。

0540

**I took my Power in my Hand**

I took my Power in my Hand—
And went against the World—
'Twas not so much as David—had—
But I—was twice as bold—

I aimed my Pebble—but Myself
Was all the one that fell—
Was it Goliah—was too large—
Or was myself—too small?

## 我畏惧寡言之人

我畏惧寡言之人——
我畏惧沉默者——
滔滔不绝的人，我将其忽略——
喋喋不休的人，我一笑置之——

但他一字千钧，当众人——
耗尽自己最后的重量——
他令我警觉——
我敬畏他的超卓——

0543

**I fear a Man of frugal Speech**

I fear a Man of frugal Speech—
I fear a Silent Man—
Haranguer—I can overtake—
Or Babbler—entertain—

But He who weigheth—While the Rest—
Expend their furthest pound—
Of this Man—I am wary—
I fear that He is Grand—

## 殉道的诗人，从不言语

殉道的诗人，从不言语——
却将剧痛锻制成音节——
当他们人世的声名凋敝——
他们必死的命运，鼓舞他人——

殉道的画家，从不说话——
却将遗赠交予，图画——
当他们停下清醒的手指——
有人在艺术中找寻，安宁之艺——

0544

**The Martyr Poets—did not tell**

The Martyr Poets—did not tell—
But wrought their Pang in syllable—
That when their mortal name be numb—
Their mortal fate—encourage Some—

The Martyr Painters—never spoke—
Bequeathing—rather—to their Work—
That when their conscious fingers cease—
Some seek in Art—the Art of Peace—

## 要弥合裂缝

要弥合裂缝
就用缺失的部分填补——
再将其封好
若用其他填充物，裂缝会加深——
你无法将深渊焊合
用空气。

0546

## To fill a Gap

To fill a Gap
Insert the Thing that caused it—
Block it up
With Other—and 'twill yawn the more—
You cannot solder an Abyss
With Air.

**0547**

## 我见过一只垂死的眼睛

我见过一只垂死的眼睛
在房间里游荡——
似乎在寻找什么——
后来它逐渐模糊——
然后,雾气迷蒙——
接着,紧紧阖上眼皮
毫不透露它见到的一切
曾经看见是一种恩赐——

0547

**I've seen a Dying Eye**

I've seen a Dying Eye
Run round and round a Room—
In search of Something—as it seemed—
Then Cloudier become—
And then—obscure with Fog—
And then—be soldered down
Without disclosing what it be
'Twere blessed to have seen—

## 我一直在爱

我一直在爱
让我给你证据
从我去爱的那天起
我从未活够——

我将永远爱着——
我向你宣告
爱是生命——
生命永不磨灭——

这一点，亲爱的，你可曾怀疑——
那么我
再没有别的能够给你
唯有我的苦难——

0549

**That I did always love**

That I did always love
I bring thee Proof
That till I loved
I never lived—Enough—

That I shall love alway—
I argue thee
That love is life—
And life hath Immortality—

This—dost thou doubt—Sweet—
Then have I
Nothing to show
But Calvary—

## 我无法证明岁月有脚

我无法证明岁月有脚——
那些已成往事的征兆
和已完成的事件
让我确信它们在跑——

我发现双脚有更远的目标——
我笑对昨天
看似完满的目标——
今天，它们的索求更多——

我毫不怀疑昔日的自我
曾与我那样相衬——
如今却已不再适合——
证明我已远超于它，我能看见——

0563

**I could not prove the Years had feet**

I could not prove the Years had feet—
Yet confident they run
Am I, from symptoms that are past
And Series that are done—

I find my feet have further Goals—
I smile upon the Aims
That felt so ample—Yesterday—
Today's—have vaster claims—

I do not doubt the self I was
Was competent to me—
But something awkward in the fit—
Proves that—outgrown—I see—

0566

## 垂死的虎，因干渴而呻吟

垂死的虎，因干渴而呻吟——
我遍寻整片沙漠——
得到一块滴水的岩石
将它捧于手中——


他威严的双目，因死而凝重——
我能看见他视网膜上
一个画面
他在寻找水，寻找我——


不应怪罪我行路太慢——
也不应怪罪他已死去
当我来到他身边时——
他的死，已成事实——

0566

## A Dying Tiger—moaned for Drink

A Dying Tiger—moaned for Drink—
I hunted all the Sand—
I caught the Dripping of a Rock
And bore it in my Hand—

His Mighty Balls—in death were thick—
But searching—I could see
A Vision on the Retina
Of Water—and of me—

'Twas not my blame—who sped too slow—
'Twas not his blame—who died
While I was reaching him—
But 'twas—the fact that He was dead—

0568

## 我们了解了爱的全部

我们了解了爱的全部——
字母，词语——
篇章，巨著——
然后，合上启示——

然而我们在彼此眼中
看见一种无知——
比年幼时更巨大——
面对面，一个孩子——

企图去阐释
他们两人都不懂得的学问——
哎，这广阔的智慧——
这复杂的真理！

0568

## We learned the Whole of Love

We learned the Whole of Love—
The Alphabet—the Words—
A Chapter—then the mighty Book—
Then—Revelation closed—

But in Each Other's eyes
An Ignorance beheld—
Diviner than the Childhood's—
And each to each, a Child—

Attempted to expound
What Neither—understood—
Alas, that Wisdom is so large—
And Truth—so manifold!

## 我忍饥挨饿，许多年来

我忍饥挨饿，许多年来——
已是正午，该就餐了——
我颤抖着拉近桌子——
伸手触摸珍奇的酒 ——

我曾多次在餐桌上见过它——
当我饥肠辘辘，走向家门
从窗外望进去，找寻财富
却无法奢望占有——

我不了解充足的面包——
它不同于糕饼屑
我常和鸟儿，分食
在大自然的饭厅里——

丰盛令我受伤，前所未有——
我感到不适与异样——
如同长于山野的莓果——
被移栽至马路上——

我不再饥饿，因而懂得

饥饿，之于窗外的人

是一种感受——

一旦入室，就可消除——

0579

## I had been hungry, all the Years

I had been hungry, all the Years—
My Noon had Come—to dine—
I trembling drew the Table near—
And touched the Curious Wine—

'Twas this on Tables I had seen—
When turning, hungry, Home
I looked in Windows, for the Wealth
I could not hope—for Mine—

I did not know the ample Bread—
'Twas so unlike the Crumb
The Birds and I, had often shared
In Nature's—Dining Room—

The Plenty hurt me—'twas so new—
Myself felt ill—and odd—
As Berry—of a Mountain Bush—
Transplanted—to the Road—

Nor was I hungry—so I found

That Hunger—was a way

Of Persons outside Windows—

The Entering—takes away—

## 害怕！我害怕谁？

害怕！我害怕谁？
不是死亡，他是谁？
不过是父亲家的门房
时常令我困窘！

害怕生命？奇怪，我畏惧
一种以一两次存在
将我包容的东西——
遵照上帝的旨意——

害怕重生？东方是否害怕
将她过于挑剔的额头
托付给黎明？
我质疑我的冠冕！

## Afraid! Of whom am I afraid?

Afraid! Of whom am I afraid?
Not Death—for who is He?
The Porter of my Father's Lodge
As much abasheth me!

Of Life? 'Twere odd I fear [a] thing
That comprehendeth me
In one or two existences—
As Deity decree—

Of Resurrection? Is the East
Afraid to trust the Morn
With her fastidious forehead?
As soon impeach my Crown!

## 我已离家多年

我已离家多年
如今站在门前
未敢踏入，生怕一张
从未见过的面孔

将我凝视
询问我在那里的事业——
"我的事业只有我余下的生命
这难道是我在那里仅存的事物？"

我倚赖着——
从前挥之不去的惶恐——
再一次如大海奔流
在我耳边爆响——

我发出碎裂的笑声
我竟惧怕一扇门
从前的我身处恐慌
也从未退缩。

我颤抖的手，小心翼翼

伸向门锁
唯恐这道可怕的门猛然向里弹开
将我拉倒在地——

我像对待玻璃一样
谨慎地缩回手指
捂上双耳，窃贼一般
喘息着从这里逃走——

0609

## I Years had been from Home

I Years had been from Home
And now before the Door
I dared not enter, lest a Face
I never saw before

Stare stolid into mine
And ask my Business there—
"My Business but a Life I left
Was such remaining there?"

I leaned upon the Awe—
I lingered with Before—
The Second like an Ocean rolled
And broke against my ear—

I laughed a crumbling Laugh
That I could fear a Door
Who Consternation compassed
And never winced before.

I fitted to the Latch

My Hand, with trembling care
Lest back the awful Door should spring
And leave me in the Floor—

Then moved my Fingers off
As cautiously as Glass
And held my ears, and like a Thief
Fled gasping from the House—

## 我无法捕捉的色彩，最好

我无法捕捉的色彩，最好——
让我拿上街市售卖——
那样缥缈的颜色
一个几尼只能看一眼——


这精美、不着痕迹的布设——
在眼中肆意铺展
像埃及艳后的侍驾——
在天空中重现——


统治的时刻
降临在灵魂之上
留下一丝精妙
难以形容的埋怨——


热切的目光，注视着风景——
仿佛它们正克制着
某种秘密，像战车
在胸膛不断地撞击——


夏日在恳求——

冬雪的小把戏——
用轻纱遮住神秘，
生怕松鼠们看穿。

它们难以捉摸，将我们嘲笑——
直到受骗的眼睛
在坟墓中傲慢地阖上——
才能以另一种方式，去看——

**The Tint I cannot take—is best**

The Tint I cannot take—is best—
The Color too remote
That I could show it in Bazaar—
A Guinea at a sight—

The fine—impalpable Array—
That swaggers on the eye
Like Cleopatra's Company—
Repeated—in the sky—

The Moments of Dominion
That happen on the Soul
And leave it with a Discontent
Too exquisite—to tell—

The eager look—on Landscapes—
As if they just repressed
Some Secret—that was pushing
Like Chariots—in the Vest—

The Pleading of the Summer—

That other Prank—of Snow—
That Cushions Mystery with Tulle,
For fear the Squirrels—know.

Their Graspless manners—mock us—
Until the Cheated Eye
Shuts arrogantly—in the Grave—
Another way—to see—

## 我们曾在一个夏日结婚

我们曾在一个夏日结婚，亲爱的——
你眼中是六月的景象——
当你短暂的生命终结，
我也厌倦了，我的——

黑暗中我寸步难行——
你就在这里将我抛下——
不知是谁带来光芒——
令我幡然醒悟。

真的，我们的未来通往殊途——
你的村舍，面朝太阳——
而我的居所
被海洋和北风四面围堵——

真的，你的花园繁花绽放，
而我，在风霜中播下种子——
那个夏日，我们都曾是女王——
但你，已在六月加冕——

0631

**Ourselves were wed one summer—dear**

Ourselves were wed one summer—dear—
Your Vision—was in June—
And when Your little Lifetime failed,
I wearied—too—of mine—

And overtaken in the Dark—
Where You had put me down—
By Some one carrying a Light—
I—too—received the Sign.

'Tis true—Our Futures different lay—
Your Cottage—faced the sun—
While Oceans—and the North must be—
On every side of mine

'Tis true, Your Garden led the Bloom,
For mine—in Frosts—was sown—
And yet, one Summer, we were Queens—
But You—were crowned in June—

## 头脑，比天空更宽阔

头脑，比天空更宽阔——
因为，将他们并排摆放——
一个能包容另一个
轻而易举，还能容纳你——

头脑比海洋更深邃——
因为，将他们对比，蓝对蓝——
一个能吸收另一个——
像海绵吸干桶中的水——

头脑与上帝分量同等——
因为，将他们称量，以磅计算——
假如差别存在的话，他们——
像音节异于声音——

0632

## The Brain—is wider than the Sky

The Brain—is wider than the Sky—
For—put them side by side—
The one the other will contain
With ease—and You—beside—

The Brain is deeper than the sea—
For—hold them—Blue to Blue—
The one the other will absorb—
As Sponges—Buckets—do—

The Brain is just the weight of God—
For—Heft them—Pound for Pound—
And they will differ—if they do—
As Syllable from Sound—

## 孩子的信仰天真

孩子的信仰天真——
完整，像他的本性——
宽阔，如同太阳初升
他纯真的眼中——
没有一丝疑虑——
会为一件小事发笑——
相信所有蒙骗
除了天国——

他坚信世界——
是自己的疆域
拥有至高无上的主权——
相形之下——
恺撒，这个卑鄙——
寡助的君王——
一无所有的统治者——
却呼风唤雨——

当他渐渐成长
对于恼人之事
他美好的估算

并不符实
令人遗憾
他学会像成年人一样——
取悦他人
而不再像国王——

0637

## The Child's faith is new

The Child's faith is new—
Whole—like His Principle—
Wide—like the Sunrise
On fresh Eyes—
Never had a Doubt—
Laughs—at a Scruple—
Believes all sham
But Paradise—

Credits the World—
Deems His Dominion
Broadest of Sovereignties—
And Caesar—mean—
In the Comparison—
Baseless Emperor—
Ruler of Nought,
Yet swaying all—

Grown bye and bye
To hold mistaken
His pretty estimates

Of Prickly Things

He gains the skill

Sorrowful—as certain—

Men—to anticipate

Instead of Kings—

## 疼痛，带着空白的要素

疼痛，带着空白的要素——
它回想不起
何时开始，或者是否存在
不痛的时候——

它没有未来，只有自身——
它的无穷包含
它的过去，在觉悟中感知
疼痛，新的时期。

0650

## Pain—has an Element of Blank

Pain—has an Element of Blank—
It cannot recollect
When it begun—or if there were
A time when it was not—

It has no Future—but itself—
Its Infinite contain
Its Past—enlightened to perceive
New Periods—of Pain.

## 我居于可能之中

我居于可能之中——
一座比散文更美妙的房屋——
拥有无数扇窗——
与精致的大门——

它那杉木搭建的厅室——
目之所及坚不可摧——
倾斜的屋顶
是无垠的天空——

最可爱的访客们——
才能将它占有——
这一片广袤拓宽我狭窄的手掌
使之聚拢天堂——

0657

**I dwell in Possibility**

I dwell in Possibility—
A fairer House than Prose—
More numerous of Windows—
Superior—for Doors—

Of Chambers as the Cedars—
Impregnable of Eye—
And for an Everlasting Roof
The Gambrels of the Sky—

Of Visitors—the fairest—
For Occupation—This—
The spreading wide my narrow Hands
To gather Paradise—

**0663**

## 他的声音又一次在门口响起

他的声音又一次在门口响起——
还是昔日的语调——
我听见他向仆人打听
一个像我这样的人——

我手捧鲜花走过去——
以此证明我就是我——
这一世我们素未谋面——
他也许会大吃一惊！

我脚步纷乱穿过厅堂——
带着沉默进门——
只见整个世界仅能容纳——
他的面庞，再无其他！

我们漫不经心地交谈——
像抛出铅锤——
一个，羞怯地试探——
另一个——
言语中的深浅——

我们一同散步，我把狗，留在家中——
温柔、体贴的月亮
和我们结伴，还没走远——
却又将我们抛下——

孤独，假如天使感到"孤独"——
当他们初次飞上天堂！
孤独，假如那些"蒙面的脸庞"，也如此感受——
他们身在天堂，无法细数！

我宁愿献出，血管中的紫红——
只为重活那一刻——
但他必须亲自数算滴落的血——
滴滴都是我的代价！

0663

**Again—his voice is at the door**

Again—his voice is at the door—
I feel the old Degree—
I hear him ask the servant
For such an one—as me—

I take a flower—as I go—
My face to justify—
He never saw me—in this life—
I might surprise his eye!

I cross the Hall with mingled steps—
I—silent—pass the door—
I look on all this world contains—
Just his face—nothing more!

We talk in careless—and in toss—
A kind of plummet strain—
Each—sounding—shyly—
Just—how—deep—
The other's one—had been—

We walk—I leave my Dog—at home—
A tender—thoughtful Moon
Goes with us—just a little way—
And—then—we are alone—

Alone—if Angels are "alone"—
First time they try the sky!
Alone—if those "veiled faces"—be—
We cannot count—On High!

I'd give—to live that hour—again—
The purple—in my Vein—
But He must count the drops—himself—
My price for every stain!

## 我们看见的就是"自然"

我们看见的就是自然——
山丘，午后——
松鼠，月圆月缺，黄蜂——
不，自然是天堂——
我们听见的就是自然——
歌雀，大海——
雷鸣，蟋蟀——
不，自然是和谐——
我们了解的就是自然——
却没有丰厚的才学去讲述——
在她的质朴面前
我们的智慧如此浅薄。

0668

**"Nature" is what we see**

"Nature" is what we see—
The Hill—the Afternoon—
Squirrel—Eclipse—the Bumble bee—
Nay—Nature is Heaven—
Nature is what we hear—
The Bobolink—the Sea—
Thunder—the Cricket—
Nay—Nature is Harmony—
Nature is what we know—
Yet have no art to say—
So impotent Our Wisdom is
To her Simplicity.

## 未来，从不言语

未来，从不言语——
也不会像一个哑人——
以手势传达一个音节
透露它将来临的深意——

然而当消息成熟——
它以行动呈现——
防止预先准备——
逃避，或替代——

嫁妆之于他——
无关紧要，就像厄运——
他的职责是给命运
发去他的电报——

0672

**The Future—never spoke**

The Future—never spoke—
Nor will He—like the Dumb—
Reveal by sign—a syllable
Of His Profound To Come—

But when the News be ripe—
Presents it—in the Act—
Forestalling Preparation—
Escape—or Substitute—

Indifferent to Him—
The Dower—as the Doom—
His Office—but to execute
Fate's—Telegram—to Him—

## 灵魂有访客

灵魂有访客
很少外出——
家中更神圣的客人——
免除了这种需要——

礼节禁止
主人离家
当人中之王
亲自到访——

0674

## The Soul that hath a Guest

The Soul that hath a Guest

Doth seldom go abroad—

Diviner Crowd at Home—

Obliterate the need—


And Courtesy forbid

A Host's departure when

Upon Himself be visiting

The Emperor of Men—

我曾啜饮生活的甘醇

## 灵魂对于自己

灵魂对于自己
仿佛尊贵的朋友——
或是敌人派来的——
一个恼人的密探——

它确保自己安全——
不惧背叛——
灵魂,是自己的君主
也因此敬畏自己——

0683

**The Soul unto itself**

The Soul unto itself
Is an imperial friend—
Or the most agonizing Spy—
An Enemy—could send—

Secure against its own—
No treason it can fear—
Itself—its Sovereign—of itself
The Soul should stand in Awe—

## 他们说"时间能够安抚"

他们说"时间能够安抚"——
时间绝不能安抚——
真实的苦难像肌腱
随着岁月愈加坚韧——

时间考验了烦恼——
却并非一种治疗——
假如它证明可以补救，也能证明
并无疾病——

0686

**They say that "Time assuages"**

They say that "Time assuages"—
Time never did assuage—
An actual suffering strengthens
As Sinews do, with age—

Time is a Test of Trouble—
But not a Remedy—
If such it prove, it prove too
There was no Malady—

0712

## 因为我无法驻足等候死神

因为我无法驻足等候死神——
他友善地停车等我——
马车里只有我们俩——
还有永生。

我们缓缓前行，他从容不迫
我将劳作与安逸
放在一旁，
以回应他的礼遇——

我们经过学校，恰逢课间
操场上，孩子们追逐玩闹——
我们经过长满稻谷的田野，凝望着——
我们经过落日——

或许，是他经过我们身旁——
冰冷的露水使我颤抖——
我穿着，单薄的裙衫——
披巾，是一层轻纱——

我们停在一座房屋前

大地仿佛在升腾——
屋顶隐约可见——
屋檐，在地面之下——


那时，仿佛已度过几个世纪，却还
不及这一天长久
我第一次猜出，马头
指向永恒——

0712

**Because I could not stop for Death**

Because I could not stop for Death—
He kindly stopped for me—
The Carriage held but just Ourselves—
And Immortality.

We slowly drove—He knew no haste
And I had put away
My labor and my leisure too,
For His Civility—

We passed the School, where Children strove
At Recess—in the Ring—
We passed the Fields of Gazing Grain—
We passed the Setting Sun—

Or rather—He passed Us—
The Dews drew quivering and chill—
For only Gossamer, my Gown—
My Tippet—only Tulle—

We paused before a House that seemed

A Swelling of the Ground—
The Roof was scarcely visible—
The Cornice—in the Ground—

Since then—'tis Centuries—and yet
Feels shorter than the Day
I first surmised the Horses' Heads
Were toward Eternity—

## 我本想到来后与她会面

我本想到来后与她会面——
死神，也有同样的计策——
可成功看似属于他——
而投降，属于我——

我本想告诉她我多期盼
这一次相逢——
可死神却抢先告诉了她——
她已随他离去——

此刻漫游就是我的歇息——
长眠，长眠就是
飓风的优待
对于记忆，对于我。

0718

**I meant to find Her when I came**

I meant to find Her when I came—
Death—had the same design—
But the Success—was His—it seems—
And the Surrender—Mine—

I meant to tell Her how I longed
For just this single time—
But Death had told Her so the first—
And she had past, with Him—

To wander—now—is my Repose—
To rest—To rest would be
A privilege of Hurricane
To Memory—and Me.

## 南风，拥有一个人

南风，拥有一个人
声音中的悲悯——
仿佛有人登陆后发现
一个移民的地址。

港口和居民的线索——
有诸多不明之处——
那更美丽的，留给远方——
留给陌生。

0719

## A South Wind—has a pathos

A South Wind—has a pathos
Of individual Voice—
As One detect on Landings
An Emigrant's address.

A Hint of Ports and Peoples—
And much not understood—
The fairer—for the farness—
And for the foreignhood.

## 戏剧最鲜活的表现是寻常生活

戏剧最鲜活的表现是寻常生活
因我们而生发——
其他悲剧

皆死于朗诵——
这是，最上等的演出
只有零星观众
演厅关闭——

"哈姆雷特"是他自己的哈姆雷特——
假如莎士比亚不曾写就——
尽管"罗密欧"没有留下
朱丽叶的记录，

演出永无穷尽
在人们心中——
这唯一有史记载的剧场
主人无法关闭——

0741

**Drama's Vitallest Expression is the
Common Day**

Drama's Vitallest Expression is the Common Day
That arise and set about Us—
Other Tragedy

Perish in the Recitation—
This—the best enact
When the Audience is scattered
And the Boxes shut—

"Hamlet" to Himself were Hamlet—
Had not Shakespeare wrote—
Though the "Romeo" left no Record
Of his Juliet,

It were infinite enacted
In the Human Heart—
Only Theatre recorded
Owner cannot shut—

## 我的生命，像一把上膛的枪

我的生命，像一把上膛的枪——
立在角落，直到有一天
主人经过，辨认出我——
并将我带走——

我们在壮阔的森林里漫游——
猎杀林间的母鹿——
每一次我替他鸣响——
群山立即回应——

我报以微笑，可亲的光芒
把山谷照耀——
仿佛维苏威式的面庞
把快乐传扬——

夜晚来临，愉快的一天结束——
我守护主人的头颅——
远比鸭绒做的软枕
更让他舒适——

谁与他为敌，就是我的死敌——

无人前来打扰——
我把黄眼睛放在他身上——
或是一根决断的拇指——

我的寿命，也许比他更久
但我必然先于他离世——
我只有权杀戮，
无权死亡——

## My Life had stood—a Loaded Gun

My Life had stood—a Loaded Gun—
In Corners—till a Day
The Owner passed—identified—
And carried Me away—

And now We roam in Sovereign Woods—
And now We hunt the Doe—
And every time I speak for Him—
The Mountains straight reply—

And do I smile, such cordial light
Upon the Valley glow—
It is as a Vesuvian face
Had let its pleasure through—

And when at Night—Our good Day done—
I guard My Master's Head—
'Tis better than the Eider—Duck's
 Deep Pillow—to have shared—

To foe of His—I'm deadly foe—

None stir the second time—
On whom I lay a Yellow Eye—
Or an emphatic Thumb—

Though I than He—may longer live
He longer must—than I—
For I have but the power to kill,
Without—the power to die—

## 预感，是草地上长长的阴影

预感，是草地上长长的阴影——
暗示太阳一个接一个落下——

告诉受惊的小草
黑暗，就要降临——

0764

**Presentiment—is that long Shadow—on the Lawn**

Presentiment—is that long Shadow—on the
Lawn—
Indicative that Suns go down—

The Notice to the startled Grass
That Darkness—is about to pass—

## 等待一个小时，太久

等待一个小时，太久——
假如爱遥不可及——
等待永无止境，不长——
假如爱终将回报——

0781

**To wait an Hour—is long**

To wait an Hour—is long—
If Love be just beyond—
To wait Eternity—is short—
If Love reward the end—

## 我无法买下，它不售卖

我无法买下，它不售卖——
世上再无其他——
我这份是唯一

我乐过头，忘记
把门关上，它便溜出去
留下我自己——

假如我能找回它，无论何地
我不介意舟车劳苦
哪怕赔上全部身家

只为望着它的眼睛——
说："你愿不愿？""你不愿。"
我便转头离去。

# I cannot buy it—'tis not sold

I cannot buy it—'tis not sold—
There is no other in the World—
Mine was the only one

I was so happy I forgot
To shut the Door And it went out
And I am all alone—

If I could find it Anywhere
I would not mind the journey there
Though it took all my store

But just to look it in the Eye—
"Did'st thou?" "Thou did'st not mean," to say,
Then, turn my Face away.

**0846**

## 夏天曾两度献给平原

夏天曾两度献给平原
她迷人的青翠——
冬天曾两度在河面上
留下银色裂缝——

秋天曾两度备下丰食
劳飨松鼠——
大自然，难道你拿不出一颗浆果
款待流浪的小鸟？

## Twice had Summer her fair Verdure

Twice had Summer her fair Verdure
Proffered to the Plain—
Twice a Winter's silver Fracture
On the Rivers been—

Two full Autumns for the Squirrel
Bounteous prepared—
Nature, Had'st thou not a Berry
For thy wandering Bird?

## 我们之间的距离

我们之间的距离
不同于路程或公海——
意志决定了它——
赤道，也无以衡量——

0863

**That Distance was between Us**

That Distance was between Us
That is not of Mile or Main—
The Will it is that situates—
Equator—never can—

## 诗人点亮的只有灯

诗人点亮的只有灯——
他们自己，熄灭——
他们使灯芯燃起——
假如生命之光

像太阳与生俱来——
每个时代是一枚透镜
播散他们的
圆周——

0883

**The Poets light but Lamps**

The Poets light but Lamps—
Themselves—go out—
The Wicks they stimulate—
If vital Light

Inhere as do the Suns—
Each Age a Lens
Disseminating their
Circumference—

## 我把自己藏进花里

我把自己藏进花里，
在你的瓶中凋落，
你，并未察觉，你感到的
几乎是一种寂寞。

0903

## I hide myself within my flower

I hide myself within my flower,
That fading from your vase,
You, unsuspecting, feel for me
Almost a loneliness.

## 假如我能让一颗心不再破碎

假如我能让一颗心不再破碎
我将不枉此生
假如我能慰藉一个生命的痛苦
抚平它的创伤

假如我能帮一只虚弱的知更鸟
重返巢穴
我将不枉此生。

0919

# If I can stop one Heart from breaking

If I can stop one Heart from breaking
I shall not live in vain
If I can ease one life the Aching
Or cool one Pain

Or help one fainting Robin
Unto his Nest again
I shall not live in Vain.

## 人可以制造言论

人可以制造言论——
言论本身很安静
却可能将导火线引向一颗火星
它正躺在蛰伏的大自然中——

让我们巧妙地，驱逐它——
让我们谨慎地，谈论它——
粉末存于火中之前——
必先存于木炭中。

0952

**A Man may make a Remark**

A Man may make a Remark—
In itself—a quiet thing
That may furnish the Fuse unto a Spark
In dormant nature—lain—

Let us deport—with skill—
Let us discourse—with care—
Powder exists in Charcoal—
Before it exists in Fire.

## 崩溃绝非一瞬之举

崩溃绝非一瞬之举
一个根本的停顿
万物崩溃
是自然朽烂的过程。

起初灵魂蒙上蛛网
表面落满灰尘
中轴被虫蛀蚀
使内在腐坏——

毁灭具有条理，魔鬼的工作
连贯而缓慢——
谁也不会，顷刻间衰败
逐步发展，崩溃之法则。

0997

## Crumbling is not an instant's Act

Crumbling is not an instant's Act
A fundamental pause
Dilapidation's processes
Are organized Decays.


'Tis first a Cobweb on the Soul
A Cuticle of Dust
A Borer in the Axis
An Elemental Rust—


Ruin is formal—Devil's work
Consecutive and slow—
Fail in an instant, no man did
Slipping—is Crash's law.

## 我们第一次知道他，身为死神

我们第一次知道他，身为死神——
第二次，身为名望——
只是第一种身份能自圆其说
第二种不能。

1006

**The first We knew of Him was Death**

The first We knew of Him was Death—
The second—was—Renown—
Except the first had justified
The second had not been.

1041

## 怀着，些许希望

怀着，些许希望，
别太遥远
那是抵挡绝望的柱顶——

怀着，些许苦痛，
别太强烈——
若有期限，也可承受。

**1041**

**Somewhat, to hope for**

Somewhat, to hope for,
Be it ne'er so far
Is Capital against Despair—

Somewhat, to suffer,
Be it ne'er so keen—
If terminable, may be borne.

## 我从未见过荒野

我从未见过荒野——
也从未见过大海——
但我知道石楠花的模样
还有那惊涛巨浪。

我从未与上帝交谈
也从未造访过天堂——
但仿佛早已得到应允
此刻我就已抵达——

1052

**I never saw a Moor 1052**

I never saw a Moor—
I never saw the Sea—
Yet know I how the Heather looks
And what a Billow be.

I never spoke with God
Nor visited in Heaven—
Yet certain am I of the spot
As if the Checks were given—

## 神圣的头衔，属于我！

神圣的头衔，属于我！
妻子，没有标志！
我被授予严峻的学位——
受难地的女皇！
至高无上，没有冠冕！
婚约在身，却没有上帝
赐予女人的痴迷——
当你拿宝石换宝石——
黄金换黄金——
出生，出嫁，入土——
一日之内完成——
三重胜利
"我的丈夫"，女人说——
弹拨着旋律——
难道这就是宿命？

1072

**Title divine—is mine!**

Title divine—is mine!
The Wife—without the Sign!
Acute Degree—conferred on me—
Empress of Calvary!
Royal—all but the Crown!
Betrothed—without the swoon
God sends us Women—
When you—hold—Garnet to Garnet—
Gold—to Gold—
Born—Bridalled—Shrouded—
In a Day—
Tri Victory
"My Husband"—women say—
Stroking the Melody—
Is this—the way?

**1078**

## 房间里的忙乱

房间里的忙乱
死后的那天清晨
是降临在人世间
最庄严的事业——

拂去心灵的杂质
把爱尘封
我们不再将它触碰
直到永生。

1078

## The Bustle in a House

The Bustle in a House
The Morning after Death
Is solemnest of industries
Enacted upon Earth—

The Sweeping up the Heart
And putting Love away
We shall not want to use again
Until Eternity.

## 生命的表象与本质

生命的表象与本质
之间的差别
就像唇间的酒
与酒罐里的酒一样大
后者，醇香可口宜储藏——
但若想一醉方休
没有瓶塞的酒才是上品——
我了解，因为我已尝过

**1101**

## Between the form of Life and Life

Between the form of Life and Life
The difference is as big
As Liquor at the Lip between
And Liquor in the Jug
The latter—excellent to keep—
But for ecstatic need
The corkless is superior—
I know for I have tried

## 1129

## 道出全部真理，但要婉转

道出全部真理，但要婉转——
成功在于迂回
对于我们脆弱的喜好
真理超凡的意外太过耀眼

就像对孩子委婉地解说闪电
以缓解他们的惊恐
真理之光须逐渐加强
否则人人都会失明——

**1129**

**Tell all the Truth but tell it slant**

Tell all the Truth but tell it slant—
Success in Circuit lies
Too bright for our infirm Delight
The Truth's superb surprise

As Lightning to the Children eased
With explanation kind
The Truth must dazzle gradually
Or every man be blind—

## 大海对小溪说"来吧"

大海对小溪说"来吧"——
小溪说"让我长大"——
大海说"你会成为一片海洋——
我要一条小溪，现在就来"！

大海对大海说"去吧"——
大海说"我就是他
你心之所爱"，"渊博的海水——
智慧对于我——如此乏味"

1210

## The Sea said "Come" to the Brook

The Sea said "Come" to the Brook—
The Brook said "Let me grow"—
The Sea said "Then you will be a Sea—
I want a Brook—Come now"!

The Sea said "Go" to the Sea—
The Sea said "I am he
You cherished"—"Learned Waters—
Wisdom is stale—to Me"

## 1212

## 当一个词脱口而出

有人说
当一个词脱口而出，
它就已死去。

我说
它正是从那天起
开始重生。

**1212**

## A word is dead

A word is dead
When it is said,
Some say.

I say it just
Begins to live
That day.

## 1222

# 我们能猜的谜

我们能猜的谜
很快遭到鄙弃——
没有陈腐的事物
只要昨日仍令人称奇——

**1222**

## The Riddle we can guess

The Riddle we can guess
We speedily despise—
Not anything is stale so long
As Yesterday's surprise—

## 假如我不曾见过太阳

假如我不曾见过太阳
原本可以承受黑暗
然而阳光已将我的荒凉
变成一种我从未见过的荒凉——

**1233**

## Had I not seen the Sun

Had I not seen the Sun
I could have borne the shade
But Light a newer Wilderness
My Wilderness has made—

## 乞丐在门前乞讨名声

乞丐在门前乞讨名声
要得到并不难
但面包比之更加神圣
施予者寥寥无几

1240

## The Beggar at the Door for Fame

The Beggar at the Door for Fame
Were easily supplied
But Bread is that Diviner thing
Disclosed to be denied

## 1263

## 没有一艘战舰能像一本书

没有一艘战舰能像一本书
带我们抵达辽远的疆土
没有一匹骏马
像腾跃的诗行——
使穷困之人免受劳苦
纵横四方——
多么廉价的战车
承载人类之灵魂。

1263

**There is no Frigate like a Book**

There is no Frigate like a Book
To take us Lands away
Nor any Coursers like a Page
Of prancing Poetry—
This Traverse may the poorest take
Without oppress of Toll—
How frugal is the Chariot
That bears the Human soul.

## 亲爱的三月，请进

亲爱的三月，请进——
我是多么高兴——
早就期盼着你——
请脱下帽子——
想必你走了很久——
这样气喘吁吁——
亲爱的三月，你好吗，还有——
你是否善待了大自然——
哦，三月，请随我上楼——
我要同你畅谈——


我曾收到你的来信，鸟儿——
枫叶却不知你已动身，直到我来报信
我宣告，它们的脸颊是多么红——
可是三月，请原谅——
你留下那些山丘，让我染上颜色——
我却找不到相配的紫——
你全都带走了——


是谁在敲门？是四月。
把门锁好——

我不愿让他追赶——
时隔一年他才来拜访
在我忙着待客的时候——
你的到来
让琐事这样微不足道

责备像赞扬一样亲切
赞扬也正像责备——

1320

**Dear March—Come in**

Dear March—Come in—
How glad I am—
I hoped for you before—
Put down your Hat—
You must have walked—
How out of Breath you are—
Dear March, how are you, and the Rest—
Did you leave Nature well—
Oh March, Come right up stairs with me—
I have so much to tell—

I got your Letter, and the Birds—
The Maples never knew that you were coming—
till I called
I declare—how Red their Faces grew—
But March, forgive me—and
All those Hills you left for me to Hue—
There was no Purple suitable—
You took it all with you—

Who knocks? That April.

Lock the Door—
I will not be pursued—
He stayed away a Year to call
When I am occupied—
But trifles look so trivial
As soon as you have come

That Blame is just as dear as Praise
And Praise as mere as Blame—

## 1340

# 一只老鼠在这里投降

一只老鼠在这里投降
一段令人愉快的短暂生涯
还有欺骗与恐惧。

耻辱也会到来
所有沉迷其中的人
请当心。

最热切的捕鼠器
无法抵抗
它想捕捉的念头——

诱惑是一个朋友
最终会厌恶地
与你分道扬镳。

1340

**A Rat surrendered here**

A Rat surrendered here
A brief career of Cheer
And Fraud and Fear.

Of Ignominy's due
Let all addicted to
Beware.

The most obliging Trap
Its tendency to snap
Cannot resist—

Temptation is the Friend
Repugnantly resigned
At last.

## 禁果有一种滋味

禁果有一种滋味
遭至合法果园的嘲弄——
被职责锁牢的豆荚里
豌豆多么甘甜多汁——

1377

## Forbidden Fruit a flavor has

Forbidden Fruit a flavor has
That lawful Orchards mocks—
How luscious lies within the Pod
The Pea that Duty locks—

### 1379

## 池塘里的华宇

池塘里的华宇
被青蛙抛弃——
他立在木桩上
发表言论——

两个世界做他的听众
但要将我除去——
四月的演说家
今已声哑——

手套戴在脚上
他没有手掌——
雄辩是泡沫
一如名声——

你报之以掌声
却在懊恼中发现
德摩斯梯尼 [1] 已消隐在
一池碧水中——

---

1　德摩斯梯尼，原文为Demosthenes，古雅典雄辩家、民主派政治家。

1379

## His Mansion in the Pool

His Mansion in the Pool
The Frog forsakes—
He rises on a Log
And statements makes—

His Auditors two Worlds
Deducting me—
The Orator of April
Is hoarse Today—

His Mittens at his Feet
No Hand hath he—
His eloquence a Bubble
As Fame should be—

Applaud him to discover
To your chagrin
Demosthenes has vanished
In Waters Green—

## 舆论总是飞掠而过

舆论总是飞掠而过，
但真理的寿命，超越太阳——
假如两者不可兼得——
那就拥有最古老的那个——

1455

## Opinion is a flitting thing

Opinion is a flitting thing,
But Truth, outlasts the Sun—
If then we cannot own them both—
Possess the oldest one—

## 1508
# 你无法让记忆生长

你无法让记忆生长
当它失去了根——
压实周围的土壤
把它扶直

也许能欺骗全世界
却救不回这棵植物——
真实的记忆像雪松
根深入坚石——

也不能砍倒记忆
一旦当它长成——
无论怎样摧残
都会萌生铁的蓓蕾——

**1508**

**You cannot make Remembrance grow**

You cannot make Remembrance grow
When it has lost its Root—
The tightening the Soil around
And setting it upright
Deceives perhaps the Universe
But not retrieves the Plant—
Real Memory, like Cedar Feet
Is shod with Adamant—
Nor can you cut Remembrance down
When it shall once have grown—
Its Iron Buds will sprout anew
However overthrown—

## 1511

## 我的祖国无须更换衣服

我的祖国无须更换衣服
她那三件式洋装[1]十分美好
就像在列克星敦[2]经过裁制
人们初次说它"合身"时那样

大不列颠对"这些星星"[3]颇为不满
流露出不易察觉的轻蔑——
他们的态度中总有什么
嘲弄着她的刺刀

1 指美国三权分立的国家体制。
2 美国马萨诸塞州东部城镇，1775年4月19日美国独立战争第一次战役在此打响。
3 指美国。美国星条旗上的星星指它的各个州。

1511

**My country need not change her gown**

My country need not change her gown,
Her triple suit as sweet
As when 'twas cut at Lexington,
And first pronounced "a fit."

Great Britain disapproves, "the stars";
Disparagement discreet,—
There's something in their attitude
That taunts her bayonet.

## 1540

## 像悲伤无所察觉

像悲伤无所察觉
夏日流逝了——
她是这样悄无声息
不似刻意叛逃——
暮色已降临很久
安静愈加纯粹
午后幽闭的时光中
大自然和自己做伴——
黄昏来得更早——
黎明焕发异彩——
像一位谦恭优雅的客人，
因离别暗自神伤——
就这样，不需一片羽翼
不用一叶扁舟
夏日迈着轻盈的脚步
与美融为一体。

1540

## As imperceptibly as Grief

As imperceptibly as Grief
The Summer lapsed away—
Too imperceptible at last
To seem like Perfidy—
A Quietness distilled
As Twilight long begun,
Or Nature spending with herself
Sequestered Afternoon—
The Dusk drew earlier in—
The Morning foreign shone—
A courteous, yet harrowing Grace,
As Guest, that would be gone—
And thus, without a Wing
Or service of a Keel
Our Summer made her light escape
Into the Beautiful.

## 1544

# 谁不曾在凡间，找到天堂

谁不曾在凡间，找到天堂——
也不会在天上获得——
因为天使会租赁房屋，与我们为邻，
不论我们迁往何处——

1544

**Who has not found the Heaven—below**

Who has not found the Heaven—below—
Will fail of it above—
For Angels rent the House next ours,
Wherever we remove—

1548

## 我们意外相逢

我们意外相逢，
有意徘徊不前——
一个世纪才有一次
如此神圣的错误
获得命运的批准，
但命运已然苍老
而且吝惜幸福
就像迈达斯[1]吝惜黄金——

---

1 迈达斯（Midas），古希腊国王，已被神化。传说他十分贪财，酒神狄俄尼索斯为
了回报他的盛情款待，赐予他点石成金的能力。

1548

## Meeting by Accident

Meeting by Accident,
We hovered by design—
As often as a Century
An error so divine
Is ratified by Destiny,
But Destiny is old
And economical of Bliss
As Midas is of Gold—

## 1549

## 我把战争存放在书里

我把战争存放在书里——
仍有一场战役——
敌人与我素未谋面
却常常将我审视——
在我与战友之间
他在犹豫，最终，
选出最精锐的斗士，把我忽略，直到
他们全体牺牲——
假如逝去的朋友不会将我遗忘
那该多么美好——
古稀之年的伙伴
毕竟屈指可数——

1549

## My Wars are laid away in Books

My Wars are laid away in Books—
I have one Battle more—
A Foe whom I have never seen
But oft has scanned me o'er—
And hesitated me between
And others at my side,
But chose the best—Neglecting me—till
All the rest, have died—
How sweet if I am not forgot
By Chums that passed away—
Since Playmates at threescore and ten
Are such a scarcity—

## 那时，垂死之人

那时，垂死之人，
清楚自己要去何处——
他们来到上帝的右手边——
那只手已被截断
上帝也不知所终——

放弃信仰
让行动变得渺小——
一点磷火照耀
胜过一片漆黑——

1551

## Those—dying then

Those—dying then,
Knew where they went—
They went to God's Right Hand—
That Hand is amputated now
And God cannot be found—

The abdication of Belief
Makes the Behavior small—
Better an ignis fatuus
Than no illume at all—

## 他饮食珍贵的言辞

他饮食珍贵的言辞——
精神因此强健——
他不再感到自己贫穷,
也不在意躯体终将入土——

他舞过黯淡的岁月
翅膀的遗赠
仅是一本书,不羁之精神
带来何等自由——

**1587**

## He ate and drank the precious Words

He ate and drank the precious Words—
His Spirit grew robust—
He knew no more that he was poor,
Nor that his frame was Dust—

He danced along the dingy Days
And this Bequest of Wings
Was but a Book—What Liberty
A loosened spirit brings—

1594

## 囚禁在天堂里!

囚禁在天堂里!
这是怎样的牢房!
让每一种束缚,
成为你最甜蜜的宇宙,
像那个曾掠夺过你的一样!

1594

**Immured in Heaven!**

Immured in Heaven!
What a Cell!
Let every Bondage be,
Thou sweetest of the Universe,
Like that which ravished thee!

1599

## 虽然大海在沉睡

虽然大海在沉睡，
它却依然深邃，
我们不能怀疑——
没有优柔寡断的上帝
点燃这片居所
再扑灭它——

1599

**Though the great Waters sleep**

Though the great Waters sleep,
That they are still the Deep,
We cannot doubt—
No vacillating God
Ignited this Abode
To put it out—

## 伊甸园是那座旧式房屋

伊甸园是那座旧式房屋
我们每天住在里面
从不怀疑自己的居所
直至被驱赶。

回望那一天，多么美好
我们信步走出家门——
并不知道折返之日，
它已无踪影。

1657

## Eden is that old—fashioned House

Eden is that old—fashioned House
We dwell in every day
Without suspecting our abode
Until we drive away.

How fair on looking back, the Day
We sauntered from the Door—
Unconscious our returning,
But discover it no more.

## 名声是多变的食物

名声是多变的食物
盛在不断更换的盘子里
这一次呈给
一位贵宾
下一次就换了对象。

乌鸦审视过谁的面包屑
并报以嘲讽的啼叫
它们展翅飞过
农民的麦粒——
人类将它们吞食，然后死去。

1659

**Fame is a fickle food**

Fame is a fickle food
Upon a shifting plate
Whose table once a
Guest but not
The second time is set.

Whose crumbs the crows inspect
And with ironic caw
Flap past it to the
Farmer's Corn—
Men eat of it and die.

## 上帝真是一个好嫉妒的神

上帝真是一个好嫉妒的神——
他无法忍受
我们将他晾在一边
彼此间却玩得不亦乐乎。

1719

## God is indeed a jealous God

God is indeed a jealous God—
He cannot bear to see
That we had rather not with Him
But with each other play.

## 我若知道第一杯是最后一杯

我若知道第一杯是最后一杯
我就该细细品尝。
我若知道最后一杯是第一杯
我就该一饮而尽。

酒杯啊,你有过错,
嘴唇并未骗我
不,嘴唇,错全在你,
幸福才是罪魁祸首。

1720

**Had I known that the first was the last**

Had I known that the first was the last
I should have kept it longer.
Had I known that the last was the first
I should have drunk it stronger.

Cup, it was your fault,
Lip was not the liar
No, lip, it was yours,
Bliss was most to blame.

## 我啜饮过生活的甘醇

我啜饮过生活的甘醇——
并告诉你我的代价——
不多不少,用尽一生——
这是市价,他们说。

他们精微地测量过我——
锱铢较量,分毫不差,
再赐予我我生命之分量——
一滴天堂的琼浆!

1725

**I took one Draught of Life**

I took one Draught of Life—
I'll tell you what I paid—
Precisely an existence—
The market price, they said.

They weighed me, Dust by Dust—
They balanced Film with Film,
Then handed me my Being's worth—
A single Dram of Heaven!

## 在我死去之前，生命已终结过两次

在我死去之前，生命已终结过两次——
却仍然无法确定
假如人能永生
是否还有第三次

如此强大，令人绝望的力量
曾两次降临于我。
不忍离别，我们无法抵达天堂，
必须离别，我们无法抗拒地狱。

1732

## My life closed twice before its close

My life closed twice before its close—
It yet remains to see
If Immortality unveil
A third event to me

So huge, so hopeless to conceive
As these that twice befell.
Parting is all we know of heaven,
And all we need of hell.

## 制造一片草原

制造一片草原，需要一株三叶草和一只蜜蜂，
一株三叶草，一只蜜蜂，
还有白日梦。
白日梦就够了，
假如连蜜蜂也没有。

**1755**

## To make a prairie

To make a prairie it takes a clover and
one bee,
One clover, and a bee,
And revery.
The revery alone will do,
If bees are few.

## 去往天堂的距离

去往天堂的距离
就像去往最近的房间
假如一位朋友正在那里等待着
幸福或厄运——

灵魂需有几多坚忍,
才足够承载
一个渐近的足音——
一扇门的开启——

1760

**Elysium is as far as to**

Elysium is as far as to
The very nearest Room
If in that Room a Friend await
Felicity or Doom—

What fortitude the Soul contains,
That it can so endure
The accent of a coming Foot—
The opening of a Door—

1761

## 火车穿过墓园大门

火车穿过墓园大门，
一只鸟张开歌喉，
啼啭，颤抖，高唱
直至响彻整个墓地；

之后它轻调曲调，
微微颔首，又唱起来。
毫无疑问，他认为此次会面
是为了向人们道别。

1761

## A train went through a burial gate

A train went through a burial gate,
A bird broke forth and sang,
And trilled, and quivered, and shook his
throat
Till all the churchyard rang;

And then adjusted his little notes,
And bowed and sang again.
Doubtless, he thought it meet of him
To say good—by to men.

## 1763

## 名声是蜜蜂

名声是蜜蜂。
它会嗡鸣——
有蜇刺——
啊，它还有翅膀。

1763

## Fame is a bee

Fame is a bee.
It has a song—
It has a sting—
Ah, too, it has a wing.

## 过于幸福的时光总会烟消云散

过于幸福的时光总会烟消云散
不留痕迹——
痛苦没有翅膀
或是太重，无法飞走——

1774

**Too happy Time dissolves itself**

Too happy Time dissolves itself
And leaves no remnant by—
'Tis Anguish not a Feather hath
Or too much weight to fly—

**1775**

## 地球有许多曲调

地球有许多曲调。
没有旋律的地方
是未知的半岛。
美是自然的真相。

但是为她的大地做证，
为她的海洋做证，
我耳中的蛩声
是她最动人的挽歌。

1775

**The earth has many keys**

The earth has many keys.
Where melody is not
Is the unknown peninsula.
Beauty is nature's fact.

But witness for her land,
And witness for her sea,
The cricket is her utmost
Of elegy to me.

# 译后记
## 没有人比她更懂得怎样去活

　　作为一名年轻的诗人和译者，重译19世纪美国传奇女诗人狄金森的作品，对我来说，是一种莫大的鼓励，我十分珍惜这次机会。狄金森的文学生涯始于她20岁的时候，她在孤独中写作30年，留下深锁在抽屉中的将近1800首没有题目的诗歌。狄金森凭借其写作的原创性和纯净性，被公认为20世纪美国现代诗的先驱之一。同时，她对中国现代诗的影响也异常深刻与持久，给众多现当代诗人的写作以灵感和启发。新版狄金森诗选——《孤独是迷人的》共收录了狄金森广为流传的160首代表作，首首经典，意蕴悠长，并以中英双语的方式呈现给广大读者。在翻译的过程中，我有许多体悟和收获，在此略写几笔，与爱诗者分享。

　　"孤独是迷人的"，这个书名起得很是贴切。一个甘于孤独的人总是充满神秘感，于孤独中向内外世界不断地探索和追问。同时，这个书名也充满力量，短短六个字精准概括出狄金森的性情及其文字卓越的气质，怎能不迷人？本书是"磨铁经典"书系"发光的女性"中的一本，也是该主题中唯一的诗集，它是磨铁图书在 2018 年夏天推出的狄金森诗选《灵魂访客》的升级版，而《灵魂访客》同样也是由我翻译的。记得 2017 年 4 月的某一天，我收到磨铁诗歌工作室主编、诗人里所的微信，她问我是否有兴趣尝试重译狄金森，为市场提供一个更为新颖与可靠的版本。对此我欣然接受。念大学时，我所学的专业就是英美文学，所以我早就接触过狄金森的诗。那时的我还无志于写作，对文本的阅读也未深入，但关于她的诗中蕴含的灵性与哲思，我一直留有深刻印象。如今，我愿意以翻译她的作品的方式重新认识和解读她。《灵魂访客》上市至今已快三年，它以坚实的文本和优质的译文赢得了众多读者的信任和青睐，豆瓣评分高达 8.4 分。在给予称赞的同时，不少读者也提出了诚恳的建议，比如希望进一步丰富诗歌的数量，以及希望增添英文原诗作为对照等，《孤独是迷人的》正是在这样的背景下应时而生的。和编辑面面女士反复商议后，我在旧版诗选的基础上增译了 30 首，并配以规范的英文原作，最终呈现出一本焕然一新的狄金森诗歌精选集，以飨读者。

我心目中的狄金森宛如诗歌精灵，永远自带光环，将她称作"发光的女性"，一点也不为过。她的诗作不仅在美国现代诗歌中具有里程碑意义，也突破了地理疆域，经得起任何时代、任何读者的审视，因为在她的诗作中，流露出的醇厚而幽深的生命感受是永恒的。狄金森生前默默无闻地写作，在忍受孤独的同时也享受着身为诗人的寂寞。她的笔能长出无数触角，触及人类生命中所能感知的方方面面，进而用文字去感受、去怀疑、去诘问、去对抗、去哀痛、去深思、去欢悦、去分享、去接纳、去共情……她用灵光闪烁的诗行建起一座诗歌华宇，每一块砖都是发光体。狄金森在诗中曾多次展现对阳光的渴求与憧憬，她的创作生涯尽管和一些文坛大家比不算漫长，但在我看来，却有着太阳般无与伦比的光辉。我且用她的一首诗加以佐证，尽管其意义指向所有诗人：

> 诗人点亮的只有灯——
> 他们自己，熄灭——
> 他们使灯芯燃起——
> 假如生命之光
>
> 像太阳与生俱来——
> 每个时代是一枚透镜
> 播散他们的
> 圆周——

翻译狄金森的诗歌的过程充满了幸福感，但我也时常深感不易，最大的困难在于吃透文本。狄金森并非传统的写作者，我想用目前国内诗歌圈的一个热词——先锋——来形容她。一个先锋诗人在思想和创作形式上常常领先于自己的时代，但绝不哗众取宠，以文本来尊重、忠于时代与个体生命，并在两者之间形成高度交融。我认为，先锋诗歌的思想远比形式重要，狄金森的诗，无论是思还是形，都堪称她所处时代的诗歌的先锋典范，放在 21 世纪的今天，仍然如此。另外，狄金森的大量诗歌都是口语写作，语言天然、简练、精确、直接，且富含哲理，比如下面这首《上帝真是一个好嫉妒的神》，全诗仅以两句话构成，句式简单易读：

> 上帝真是一个好嫉妒的神——
>
> 他无法忍受
>
> 我们将他晾在一边
>
> 彼此间却玩得不亦乐乎。

狄金森的一部分诗运用了口语化的常规句式，读起来朗朗上口；还有相当一部分，在形式上别具一格，对传统句式多有改造和颠覆。首先，她并不固守传统的音韵格律。她的许多作品看似是典型的四行诗，采用圣歌或民谣体，却蕴含大量的变化和实验因素，比如以破折号代替各种标点，并突破常规断句，产生新的节奏感，仿佛骑上马背，一时疾行、一时腾跃、一时突停。其次，狄金森的诗都无标题，诗行中遍布不规则的大写字母，在韵脚上也不严格，擅用半韵（slant rhyme）。一些断句甚至不受行数限制，单独成节，以至于读惯四行体的人可能会将之视为排版错误，比如书中这首《美，不经雕琢，与生俱来》：

> 美，不经雕琢，与生俱来——
>
> 若去追逐，它必闪躲——

顺其自然，它将永驻——

超越时光

牧场上，当风的手指
轻抚过草地——
神赐予的美
你永远无法造就——

　　这首诗的第四句单独成节，这样的安排引起了学术界的讨论，但至今尚无定论。再次，除了句式上的理解困难，狄金森对词序的任意颠倒，是译者和读者面临的又一挑战。在翻译中，我常感觉她像个任性的孩子，喜爱玩积木，随兴致任意丢放木块，造出谜一样的形体，令人惊讶。读者挖空心思解谜，但谁也不敢笃定自己的结论是正确的，怕是只有进入天堂得以面见诗人，才能问个清楚吧。

　　除去形式的先锋，狄金森思想之"渊深"（江枫先生语），也令人惊叹。她的写作题材广阔，涉及自然、生活、死亡、信仰、灵魂、哀痛、战争，以及科学等。那些表面上看似简练的诗歌，却蕴含丰裕的知识、深奥的哲理、玄妙的隐喻与复杂矛盾的情感。

　　狄金森是她的家族中唯一不信教的人，甚至对上帝颇有质疑。也许是因为她的成长环境，也许是因为她终生都沉迷于对死亡的探索，她在诗中常提到上帝，并与之对峙。她关于死亡与信仰的书写，常有奇思，比如这首《埋进坟墓的人们》，首句便提出质疑："埋进坟墓的人们／都会朽烂吗？"诗人以其觉知，否认自己的死亡，并以耶稣的名义说："有一种人存在／他们永远尝不到死的滋味——"结尾托出诗的高潮，令人拍案叫绝："我无须再做争辩／上帝的话／不容置疑／他告诉我，死亡已死——"译到这里，我很自然地想到尼采的超人理论"上帝已死"，两者在精神上有着不谋而合的伟大。我还有另一种合情的推理，即狄金森的内心其实是信仰上帝的，但她会质疑、追问死之后事。谁也难以回答这个问题，但每一种宗教下，都有人追问，并由此形成自己的信仰体系。我想这就是狄金森的诗歌能同时被不同信仰、不同性别、不同文化背景下的人所接受的原因。我也由此理解，为何她常年隐居，并终身不婚。与世隔绝使她饱受折磨，但也成就了她最伟大的精神体验。她最令我动容的，就是超越环境的自觉性思考：上帝完全可能不存在，不管她的父亲，她的家庭，她的学校，她所生活的新英格兰给她怎样的压力，她都如此坚信着。她的诗歌就是要对世界说：这是我的想法，我毫不介意你们怎么想！狄金森关于自然的诗歌也承载了她的思索精神，她眼中的自然并非来自上帝的荣耀创造，而更像她的观察对象。她的诗歌对自然进行了细致而冷静的观察，因此非常独立、精确和超然。她仿佛将一双无形又谦逊的眼睛安放在上帝之上，以其记录万物存在的奥秘，等有缘之人领悟。

有时，遇上一首并不算长的难译的诗歌，我要读上两三天，逐一推敲被打乱的语序，查阅大量的一手资料，才得领悟。这种阅读时的难以通达，除了与她的思想有关，应该还和她研究过17世纪英国玄学派诗歌有关。玄学派诗人善于营造新奇的意象，特别喜欢使用那些用于形容迥异事物之间关联的暗喻。比如17世纪的玄学派诗人约翰·多恩，在《别离辞：节哀》这首诗里创造了一个著名比喻，是将一对恋人比作圆规的两只脚："你的灵魂是定脚，并不像／移动，另一脚一移，它也动"（卞之琳译）。我想狄金森继承了玄学诗新颖奇异的写法，加之天赋异禀，她写得更为灵动、丰富和幽深。她的诗歌中的种种隐喻、象征与通感，十分奇崛，又很自然，像是万物自然生发，瓜熟蒂落。但有些修辞也难免晦涩，甚至不可译，因此各个译本差异很大，研究狄金森的文论家之间时常产生分歧也很正常。

以爱为主题的诗歌，当然也包括情诗。这类诗歌在狄金森的众多诗作中占有很大的比重，不仅有写给某一位爱人的，还有写给家人、挚友的。她被世人冠以"阿默斯特修女"的称呼，再加上常年离群索居，身上似乎多了一种神圣不容亵渎，或者说不食人间烟火的色彩。但若深入阅读她的情诗，你不难被其中不断涌动的生气和炽烈打动。她比她身边的任何一个人，都更敢于去活，也更懂得生而为人的情感。这些诗给人带来敏锐的触觉，天真与精微并存，仿佛可以穿在身上，虽然安静，却让人无法忽视其自带的温度与重量。假如要用一种布料来形容，那就是亚麻，根植在阴凉的土地上。它没有棉的软塌无骨，也无需丝绸的明艳。它自带生动凸凹的纹理、宁静的光泽和一种略带冒犯的粗粝。仔细抚触，它在亲肤的同时，也给你以柔韧。比如这首《月亮离海很远》的最后一节，有一种夜风从布缝中吹过的清凉与温柔：

> 哦，先生，你那，琥珀色的手——
> 还有我的，遥远的海——
> 你任何一个目光的授意
> 都将令我唯命是从——

她的情诗也带有岩石的冷峻和尊严，严肃、深沉，引而不发，例如《灵魂选择她自己的侣伴》，她在首节写下：

> 灵魂选择她自己的侣伴——
> 然后，关上门——
> 忠于内心神圣的选择——
> 不再抛头露面——

她也写过浓烈的情诗，带有火的灼伤，令人躲避不及，比如这首著名的《暴风雨夜》，她在首节直抒内心：

> 暴风雨夜，暴风雨夜！
> 你若在我身边
> 狂风暴雨中
> 我们将共度春宵！

这首诗中最关键的一个词就是第一节中的"luxury"，现在多译为"奢华"，但在一百多年前，它的旧义直指"肉欲",其意义也与末节最后两句"今夜,我只想停泊/在你深处"吻合。有意思的是,这首写于1861年的诗,当年被拒绝发表,其中一个原因就是它与诗人的修女形象不符,有亵渎感。一个诗人,首先要是一个完整的人,若没有七情六欲,写出的东西也未必值得读者去读。

关于我的译本,我也想略说几点。狄金森的英文原诗在图书市场及网络上都有不少版本流传,在用词、行文、标点、诗歌编号和断行等方面存在不同程度的差异。为了文本的严谨和统一,本书的英文原诗参考的是业界权威版本之一——1976年1月由托马斯·约翰逊(Thomas H. Johnson)编辑、利特尔&布朗出版社出版的《艾米莉·狄金森诗全集》(以下简称《全集》),诗歌编号全部采用约翰逊的编号方式。即便如此,《全集》里部分诗歌的体貌仍给我们留下不少探讨的空间,让我印象深刻的有两首。第216首《安然无恙地睡在玉室里》,《全集》提供了1859年和1861年两个版本,除去格式上的差别,诗歌第二节的内容全然不同。也许是兴之所至,也许是阅历和感受有所变化,狄金森给了这首诗两种不同的结尾。我选译的是1861版,因为我感觉这个版本中诗意的递进更加自然,意象也更奇崛。此外,第903首《我把自己藏进花里》也给了我小小的"意外",因为编辑告诉我原诗只有四行,而我译了八行。这首诗歌在《全集》中的版本是一首"绝句",而不是当初我在谷歌上找到的"律诗"。这里不妨贴上我最初的译文,供大家品评:

我把自己藏进花里

让你戴在胸口

你，并未察觉，你戴着我——

可天使知道一切


我把自己藏进花里，

在你的瓶中凋落，

你，并未察觉，你感到的

几乎是一种寂寞。


关于狄金森诗歌中破折号太多的问题，我在本书中也进行了优化。为了让读者拥有更为舒适与流畅的阅读感受，我删除了句中多处破折号，以逗号代替，句末的破折号仍然依照原文保留，这种做法既保存了诗意的自然停顿，也尊重了现代读者的阅读习惯。这一点改进也有一位豆瓣读者的功劳，他没有给《灵魂访客》打高分，理由是书籍里过多的破折号让他几次拿起书想读，又不得不放下，破折号使他的阅读非常卡顿，无法继续。感谢他中肯的意见，希望不久之后，他有机会读到这本全新的诗集，重获美好的体验。

关于译本的特色，我想做如下说明：我本身是一个诗人，所以不太愿意以理论家或翻译家的口吻谈论狄金森，更多的是想从一个诗人的角度，从文本的层面来解读她。我热爱她，在翻译的同时，也写下了类似译后感的诗。假如可能的话，我更愿意在翻译时，以一个后辈诗人的身份，在精神世界里穿越时空感受她、成为她。我相信这样能够增强译本的可信度，这也是我信任的一种翻译方式。此外，我在前文中提过，狄金森的诗歌多使用半韵，但我力求译得更传神和贴切，所以没有考虑押韵的因素，也不想受其约束。

最后，我想向一些同行和朋友致谢。首先，我要对沈浩波先生和里所女士致以诚挚的谢意，没有他们的信任与支持，就没有《灵魂访客》的诞生和《孤独是迷人的》的延续，特别感谢沈浩波先生为这本新书慷慨献言，奉上一篇精彩绝伦、字字珠玉的导语。其次，我也要感谢磨铁大鱼优秀的编辑面面女士耐心细致的沟通，以及孙佳怡女士异常辛苦的编校工作。假如这本书有幸获得成功，这其中必定包含以上每一位的付出与厚爱！今后若有机会，我依然愿意为一切优秀的英文诗歌服务，提供高品质的翻译。再次，感谢各位前辈翻译家，他们已经在文本上做出了极其卓越的贡献，让我受益良多，也给我的翻译提供了珍贵的参考价值。我非常愿意以我的新译本与各位前辈做进一步的交流与学习。

最后的最后，我想以我的一首诗，结束这篇译后记，并向狄金森本人以及热爱她的读者们致以敬意：

**唯一**

没有人

演得好

狄金森

演得好

那样一个

十几年

足不出户

只在一个夜里

悄然出行

借着月光

去看一座

新教堂

的人

**苇欢**

2021/06/18

于广东珠海